The Warm Place

A Richard Jackson Book

THE WARM PLACE

by Nancy Farmer

Orchard Books · New York

Orchard Books, 95 Madison Avenue, New York, NY 10016

Manufactured in the United States of America
Book design by Mina Greenstein
The text of this book is set in 12 point Sabon.
1   3   5   7   9   10   8   6   4   2

Library of Congress Cataloging-in-Publication Data
Farmer, Nancy.
The Warm Place / by Nancy Farmer.   p.   cm.
"A Richard Jackson book"—Half t.p.
Summary: When Ruva, a young giraffe, is captured and
sent to a zoo in San Francisco, she calls upon two rats,
a street-smart chameleon, a runaway boy, and all
the magical powers of the animal world to return
to the warm place that is home.
ISBN 0-531-06888-9.   ISBN 0-531-08738-7 (lib. bdg.)
[1. Giraffes—Fiction.   2. Home—Fiction.   3. Animals—
Fiction.   4. Poaching—Fiction.   5. Zoos—Fiction.]
I. Title.   PZ7.F23814War   1995
[Fic]—dc20   94-21984

TO MY MOTHER

$\mathcal{O}ne$

IN A GAME PARK in central Africa lived a herd of giraffes. One morning, at the beginning of the rainy season, a mother giraffe gave birth to a baby. She named her Ruva.

Ruva looked around at the grassland and the forest at its edge. Until then, all she had known was darkness. "What is it?" she asked.

"That is the World," her mother replied.

"What is the World?"

"Everything you see."

"How big is it?" the little giraffe asked.

"Goodness! I don't know. If you walk one day in that direction and one day in this direction, you will cover most of it. Now go to sleep," said Mother.

How did Ruva and her mother talk? They stood

just so and moved just so. They waved their ears and blinked their eyes. They wriggled their noses and swished their tails. In these and a thousand other ways, they spoke the Common Speech. It was the language with which Noah called the animals to the ark.

For the first week, Ruva sat under a bush while Mother guarded her. "The first task you must learn is to grow," Mother told her. "Don't walk around. Walking uses up energy. Lie still and grow."

Ruva watched her aunts and uncles move in stately groups across the grassland. Sometimes they disappeared right before her eyes. One moment she saw a group of giraffes feeding at a tree. The next moment she saw a group of trees standing all together.

"What happened to them?" she asked.

"That is Giraffe Magic," said Mother. "You will learn it when you're older."

After the first week, the tiny horns that had lain flat against Ruva's skull sprang up. They were soft and tufted with hair. Ruva was allowed to leave her hiding place under the bush.

She followed her aunts and uncles as they fed. Sometimes the uncles got into arguments. They swung at one another with their long necks and said insulting things. "Why are you angry?" asked Ruva. "What does *long-necked, mangy, flea-infested idiot* mean?"

"Mind your own business," said the uncles.

"Those are Grown-up Matters," Mother explained. "You will learn about them later."

Ruva explored under the trees. She came to a large patch of shade that smelled of crushed grass. She sniffed at it, and the shade turned into a buffalo that waved its heavy horns as it walked away. "Don't bother others when they're taking a nap," the buffalo called over its shoulder.

Ruva discovered a long, flat rock in the reeds next to the river. She tried to climb it with her sharp little hooves. "Watch where you're going!" bellowed the hippo as it stood up. It slid into the river and floated there with its eyes and nose above the water.

"That is Buffalo and Hippo Magic," Mother said. "Those animals won't hurt you if you bump into them, but the lion, leopard, and hyena will. They have Magic, too. You had better learn about it right now, or they will gobble you up, hoof, horn, and hide."

So Ruva learned how tawny, golden grass could turn into lion. She learned how speckled shadow could become leopard and how the slidy shadow of the rocks hid the hyena. She learned these lessons well. She didn't want to be gobbled up, hoof, horn, and hide!

But there was one thing Mother couldn't protect her from. "Humans are the sneakiest creatures alive," Mother said. "They look like hairless monkeys and smell like dead hyenas. They have forgotten the Common Speech. *We* can understand *them*.

They have no more idea of us than an earthworm has of the sky."

"They're asleep, like the tortoise," said Ruva.

"The tortoise isn't asleep, my darling." Mother paused to nibble an acacia tree. Her long tongue cleverly plucked out the tender leaves from between the thorns. "Tortoise is one hundred years old. He has said all he cared to say long ago. Humans are different."

Ruva's neck was just long enough to reach the acacia. She, too, picked out leaves from between the thorns and added a pod for flavor.

"Humans are forever meddling with things," Mother said. "Leaves, trees, mountains, you name it—before you can say *ouch*, they have broken them. That's stupidity. But humans also know a thousand tricks, and they love to play them on us. All I can tell you is this: if you see something you have never seen before—and it smells like a dead hyena—run for your life!"

RUVA was walking at the edge of the forest when she saw an odd thing. It wasn't leaves; it wasn't grass. It was a bright green flower in the darkest part of the forest.

She looked back to see Mother and one of her aunts sharing a paperbark tree out on the grassland. "I should tell them where I'm going. They're so far away, though." Ruva looked for tawny, golden grass and speckled shadows and slidy shadows. She didn't see any.

She stepped onto the trail. Dragonflies darted from under her feet. Butterflies fluttered past her ears. And there it was, hanging like a green leafy ball over the trail.

How can that be? she wondered. Flowers don't float. Mother's words came back to her: *if you see something you have never seen before—and it smells like a dead hyena—run for your life!* She sniffed the air, which was almost still under the dense dark trees. Nothing.

I wonder what it tastes like, thought Ruva. It can't hurt—to lean out—like this—

She took a step forward and *snap!* A net exploded from the leaves and swept her off her feet. "Mother! Mother!" bleated the little giraffe. The net swung back and forth. The lettuce broke off its string and rolled under her feet.

Horrible hairless monkeys jumped out of the shadows, and now she did smell them! They grinned at her with terrible flat teeth as they dragged her along the trail.

"Mother! Mother!" Ruva cried.

From far away she heard Mother call, "I'm coming!"

"Hurry up before the game rangers catch us!" shouted one of the humans.

"Give this animal a shot. She's half-dead of fright," said another. Ruva felt a sting. She was

[5]

hauled onto something that roared as it charged off. She saw Mother racing through the trees, but the hairless monkeys went even faster. The sky turned over, a black cloud came down, and then Ruva was fast asleep.

Two

SHE AWOKE in a large room filled with alarming shapes. Bunches of bananas loomed on one side of her cage, with nets full of coconuts on the other. The coconuts rolled from side to side as the floor moved.

The movement made her sick. A spray of acacia leaves was tied to the bars of the cage. She was unable to eat it.

Time passed. The light in the room went from shadowy to very dark to shadowy again. The coconuts rolled; the bananas shifted. The humans visited her, which was very frightening indeed. They pried open her mouth to give her milk. Ruva spat it back at them. After a while, they left her alone with a heap of vegetables and a trough of water.

She lapped at the water. It tasted stale. She knew

the humans were only keeping her until they became hungry. Then they would fall on her with their terrible flat teeth. She closed her eyes and waited for death.

"You dodo. When people offer *me* food, I say, 'Thank you very much,' and eat it," a sharp voice said, not far from her ear.

Ruva opened her eyes. There, perched among the bananas, was a large rat. He wasn't quite like the cane rats of the forest, but he was clearly a relative. "Who are you?" she asked.

"*I,*" said the rat with a flourish of his tail as he climbed down the bananas, "am Rodentus von Stroheim the Third, world citizen and traveler. I have partied with presidents, roistered with rajas, and dined with the Dalai Lama. You may call me Rodentus."

None of this made sense to Ruva, but she was glad of a familiar animal face. "I am Ruva, a giraffe," she said. She couldn't think of anything more impressive to say.

"Well, Ruva-a-Giraffe, what are you going to do about your problem?" The rat drew himself up on hind legs and studied her. He had a beautiful coat that reminded her of tawny, golden grass. His paws were neat and his vibrissae well-groomed.

"I don't know what my problem is," said Ruva.

"Well, then, I'll tell you. You have been captured by the Slope Siblings. They'll do anything so long as it's evil. They sell tropical-rain-forest firewood and panda-bear hatbands. They haul nuclear waste to South Sea islands and make them glow brighter than the full moon. At the moment, they are taking you to a zoo where ugly little humans called children will throw popcorn at you."

Ruva was confused by all this. She thought she was going to be *devoured* by little humans. They would soften her up first by pelting her with popcorn. She closed her eyes and moaned.

"Stop that!" cried Rodentus, covering his ears.

"Does it—does it take a long time to be softened up with popcorn?" moaned Ruva.

"You ninny! They want to keep you as a *pet*. I would call it slavery, however. It is the duty of all slaves to escape. I expect you to try, so stop sniveling. I have no patience with cowards."

"But what can I do?" Ruva wailed.

"Eat, for one thing. You won't get far if you can't walk."

And so the little giraffe thought about food for the first time since she was kidnapped. She found the dry branch of acacia and ate it because it was familiar. The taste brought back memories of the grassland, and Mother. . . .

"Moping is *not* acceptable," said Rodentus in a sharp voice. "You have perfectly good giraffe food there. Personally, I think salads are for sissies, but that's because I'm a rat. The right dressing does wonders. I had a meal with the raja of Mysore—great salad man, the raja—vegetarian, you know—now *he* had a salad dressing of mango, lemon juice, and coconut oil. . . ."

As he talked, Rodentus offered Ruva samples of vegetables. She ate unwillingly at first, but suddenly her appetite came back with a rush.

"Whoa! Don't eat *me!*" the rat exclaimed as Ruva lunged at a spinach leaf. "That's spinach. Good for energy. I suppose you didn't taste it, it went down so fast. That's lettuce—*now* what's wrong?"

Ruva spat out the leaf. "They used lettuce to trap me. I shall never eat it. Never."

"Quite right. Disgusting stuff. Try this carrot." With coaxing and threats, Rodentus got the little giraffe to eat every scrap of food in her cage. Except the lettuce.

Ruva had starved herself so long, the large meal made her sleepy. She leaned against the bars in a contented daze.

A sailor opened a hatch in the ceiling and looked down at her. "Hey, Captain!" he called. "The little beastie finally ate her greens."

A flat ugly face appeared at the hatch. "Thought she would," it said. "Animals respond well to starvation. It's my opinion you can teach an elephant to tap-dance if you starve and beat it long enough."

"Yes, Captain," said the sailor. The hatch closed.

Rodentus was hidden in the shadows. His lips were curled and his teeth chattered. He no longer seemed like a gentleman who had compared salad dressings with the raja of Mysore. He looked like a bilge rat on a pirate ship.

Ruva was shocked. "Are you all right?"

"Yes—*chchchch*—yes—oh, drat—*chchchch*—he always does that to me." Rodentus bit himself on the paw. "Ow! That's better. I tell you, I can't help myself when I see one of them."

"Who?"

"A *Slope*. The sailors are all right—for humans—but their bosses are the lowest form of life on earth. They're *demons*. The father of the clan is Slippery Slope, who owns a fleet of ships. His oldest daughter is Synthia. Then there's Spongy, Stonewall, Sargon, and Skeekee." The rat made an ugly sound that alarmed Ruva.

"Are you sick?" she asked.

"That's how you say his name: *Skeekee*. That's the monster who looked down at us. When you say his name right, it sounds like someone scraping his fingernails across a blackboard." The rat sat down in the rounded bowl formed by a bunch of bananas. His shoulders hunched with depression.

"Maybe you should come with me when I escape," Ruva suggested.

Rodentus laughed bitterly. "I'm on an assignment. I can't leave."

"If I could get out of this cage, I could go home right now." Ruva nosed the bars and tugged them with her mouth. "Mother said that if you walked one day in that direction and one day in this direction, you would cover most of the World. It shouldn't take long."

The rat stared at her for a moment. "I hate to

criticize anyone's mother, but she was slightly off with her measurements."

"What do you mean?" said Ruva with a flutter of alarm.

"I mean we're on a ship in the middle of the ocean. There's a thousand miles of water between us and Africa. It shouldn't take you more than a year to swim home."

Ruva was so overcome by this news, she stretched out her neck and bawled. "Boagh! Boagh! I'll never see Mother again! Boagh!"

"Be quiet. Do you want the humans to hear you?"

"I don't care! Boagh!"

"Well, I do. Here you have the most brilliant, talented teacher in the World. I could train that knobby little mind of yours into something wonderful—and all you can do is bleat!"

"I can't help it! Boagh!"

"Shut up or I'll tell Skeekee to tenderize you with popcorn."

Ruva fell silent at once. A sailor opened the hatch and peered down at them. Ruva sat perfectly still with Rodentus hidden in her shadow. The hatch closed.

"Lie down, Ruva-a-Giraffe," said the rat. "Your uncle Rodentus is going to tell you a bedtime story."

Three

"I HEARD THIS while dining with the pope in Rome," Rodentus began. He settled himself into a coil of rope by the cage.

"What's a pope? What's a Rome?" asked Ruva.

"Later. Pay attention to the story. The pope was entertaining a monk from the deserts of Egypt. This person understood the Common Speech—"

"Do humans know the Common Speech?" interrupted Ruva.

"A few. I shouldn't have let you eat that spinach. It made you too talkative."

"I'll be quiet," promised the little giraffe.

"Thank you. Now as I was saying . . ."

THE HISTORY OF THE TOWER OF BABEL
From the Animals' Point of View

It started with the mice. There were far too many of them in the land of Shinar. They ate the grain and swam in the milk jugs. They nibbled the bread and made nests of fine woolen cloth.

"Cursed mice!" shouted the people of Shinar. They caught them in baskets.

"Please, Noble Great Ones," squeaked the mice. "We are a people like you, with children who cry if they are not fed. If you kill us, they will starve. Think of your own babies. How would you like *them* to lie in an empty house without any food?"

So the people of Shinar turned the mice loose. It was hard to kill animals when you understood their point of view.

Then the rats began to gnaw holes in the grain bins. The wild pigs dug up the crops. The gophers devoured the roots. The cattle refused to give milk if their calves still wanted it, and the hens refused to surrender their eggs. The animals always had good reasons for their behavior, and the people of Shinar took pity on them.

Now the king of Shinar was a mighty hunter called Nimrod. When he walked into the forest, he was exactly equal to the lions he hunted. They had claws and teeth; he had a sword and spear. It was fitting that they hunt each other. Nimrod always came home with a lion, instead of the other way around, because he had more courage.

King Nimrod was the bravest man alive, but he wasn't intelligent. That hardly mattered with the lions. They, too, were brave and not loaded with brains.

The people of Shinar went to Nimrod and said, "Tell us what to do about the animals. The rats and mice have been up to mischief, and the wild pigs and gophers as well. Also, our cattle refuse to give milk, and the hens peck us when we try to take their eggs. We don't know what to do."

Nimrod thought and thought. It looked impressive, but inside he was thinking: I wonder what's for lunch. I want to try that new polish on my spear. My ankle itches.

"Give us advice, O Mighty One," cried the people. Nimrod sat back on his throne. He glared at each person in turn, but inside he was thinking: What advice? What question did they ask?

A courtier who knew the king better than anyone said, "What shall we do about our quarrel with the animals?"

Aha! thought Nimrod, remembering. "If the animals bother you," he said aloud, "tell them to go away. There, I've given you advice. Now shoo!"

"How can we send them away?" said the people outside the palace.

The courtier explained. "Let us build a wall and put all the animals outside. Turn them loose to see how they like it. When we finally let them come home, they'll be so grateful, they'll give us all their milk and eggs."

So the people of Shinar built a round wall. Inside was a spring of water and enough land to plant crops. They put all the chickens, cattle, goats, and sheep outside. They drove away the mice, rats, wild pigs, and gophers.

For a while, all was peaceful. Then the mice burrowed holes in the wall. They were followed by the gophers. When a wild pig tumbled out onto a bed of melons, the people of Shinar built a stronger, higher wall inside. There was peace for a while until the mice broke through again.

It went on like this, with the walls getting higher and the land inside getting smaller, until the humans were crowded into a jumble of houses at the center. By then they had named the new town Babel. They began to build upward. The mice followed, chewing their way through the floors.

Higher and higher rose the tower of Babel. Finally, the mice gave up. The people of Shinar lived at the top of the tower for a long time. They saw no animals except the eagles, who floated high overhead and did not care to speak with anyone.

When they had eaten all the stored food, the people climbed down, broke open the walls, and came out again into the broad, green World.

"Come here!" they called to the cattle, sheep, chickens, and goats.

Moo! said the cattle, rolling their eyes.

Bah! said the goats, lowering their horns.

In the end, the people had to run around and catch them. They had to pen them with fences so they wouldn't run away. The animals understood very well what the humans wanted. They ran like deer because they liked their freedom.

The humans had forgotten the Common Speech during the time they spent in the tower of Babel. Because they couldn't understand the animals' point of view anymore, they took all the milk and eggs they wanted. They killed the mice and rats without pity.

King Nimrod, who had not joined them in the tower, was long gone. He had been taken home by a lion who turned out to be smart as well as brave. The people chose the courtier to be their new king.

"Since that time, humans have been ignorant of the Common Speech," Rodentus said.

"Except for a few," Ruva murmured sleepily.

"You remembered." The rat was pleased.

"That was a good story—oh, ahh." The little giraffe yawned and stretched.

"Infants are born knowing the Speech. They forget it when they learn to talk like humans—but not all," the rat said softly. "Not all." Ruva's long eyelashes drooped. She sighed and snuggled against the hard floor. In a moment she was asleep.

Rodentus climbed an air vent to the deck. He slunk along to the captain's quarters. It was night, and untidy heaps of rope, fishing gear, and old rum bottles made it easy to hide. The door was open in the tropical heat.

Inside, Captain Skeekee drank with his brother Spongy and his sister Stonewall. Spongy was a mass of rippling fat tucked into a sailor's uniform. Stonewall was six and a half feet tall and looked as though she ought to have bolts in her neck. She neither spoke nor smiled. Spongy and Skeekee discussed their next project.

Rodentus von Stroheim the Third listened intently. He clenched his teeth to keep them from chattering.

Four

THE RAT WAS a stern teacher. Many a lesson ended in tears as poor Ruva tried to remember the chief products of France or the nine-times table.

"Stop quivering like a marshmallow," ordered Rodentus, marching up and down like a drill sergeant. "Your education has been woefully neglected. You must have grown up in a cave."

"But what *good* is it?" Ruva cried. "None of my relatives were educated, and they were perfectly happy."

"I don't doubt that your relatives lived in happy ignorance. They didn't have to escape slavery and travel halfway around the World. I don't know which of these facts will come in handy, so you'd better learn them all."

"I can't!" wailed Ruva.

"Piffle! The son of the Japanese emperor studies sixteen hours a day. He loves every minute of it."

"You visited the emperor of Japan?"

"We had the most divine sushi. Don't change the subject."

But the little giraffe couldn't go on. She began to bang her head against the bars of her cage. "Hate France"—*bang*—"hate nine-times table"—*bang*—"hate sushi, whatever that is"—*bang*—

"Stop that!" shouted Rodentus. "You've made your point. You're going stir-crazy. It's no wonder, a free animal locked up in a tiny cage—ought to be a law. There *is* a law, but no one obeys it." Muttering to himself, the rat climbed the bars, inserted his tail into the lock, and clicked it open. The door swung wide.

Ruva was so startled, she didn't realize what had happened for a moment. She stared at the door as Rodentus climbed down and flexed the tip of his tail. "How did you do that?" she whispered.

"Picked the lock, obviously."

"You knew all along how to open the door?"

"All us rats are natural lock pickers."

"Then why didn't you do it earlier?" Ruva burst into tears. She wept as she had never done before, not even when she was captured.

Rodentus watched her anxiously. Finally, when her sniffles died away, he said, "I'm sorry. I was afraid. You didn't know anything about the World. You didn't know what a ship was or an ocean. I thought you might walk right over the side. Or be caught by Skeekee—*chchchch*—and chained up."

The rat climbed the bars until he was on a level with Ruva's face. "You think it's bad in a cage? You could be in a cage *and* chained. Skeekee might beat you. He loves doing things like that. I couldn't take the chance." Rodentus reached out and patted Ruva on the nose. She sighed deeply.

"You can walk around the hold now. Every night and every afternoon the sailors are either sleeping, drugged, drunk, or all three. I know their habits. Come on, my dear. Take a stroll for Uncle Rodentus."

So Ruva left the cage for the first time. She stepped around boxes marked

DANGER! EXPLOSIVES!
WEAR GAS MASK WHEN OPENING.

She put her ear against the hull and listened to the engines. The walk cheered her immensely.

"The Slopes can't be all bad," she remarked, looking around at the cargo. "They sell coconuts and bananas."

The rat laughed harshly. "The coconuts are infested with beetles, and the bananas have blight. Some poor third-world country will buy them. The beetles will eat their trees, and blight will kill their crops. Count on it. If the Slopes are involved, it's wicked."

Ruva was unwilling to reenter the cage, but Rodentus was firm. "The sailors wake up around now—with hangovers, I hope. They mustn't find you out. Don't worry. I'll free you again."

The little giraffe helped close the door with her hoof and held it while the rat worked the lock. "Did you really have meals with all those famous humans?" she asked.

"Not all of them were *aware* I was sharing their food," said Rodentus in a rare burst of honesty. "The Dalai Lama did feed me rice crackers. He's a fine man."

T HE DAYS passed almost pleasantly. Ruva learned facts until she thought her head would swell. Rodentus let her out when the sailors were sleeping. He often disappeared on mysterious missions but never left her alone too long. Twice a day, food and water were brought by a sailor who scratched her between the horns and said she was "a bonny beastie."

The coconuts and bananas were unloaded at an unsuspecting third-world port. They were replaced with T-shirts guaranteed to shrink.

And then the unthinkable happened. One day the ship docked—Ruva heard the anchor chain rattle out. She wondered which poor souls would get the shrinking T-shirts. The hatch opened; a big crane reached down and plucked up Ruva's cage faster than a striking hawk.

"Rodentus! Help!" she bleated.

"I didn't know they were unloading you here," panted the rat as he climbed the bundles of T-shirts. "Come with me!"

"I can't! Escape! Go home! Never give up!" That was all Rodentus was able to say before the cage was swung up into the light and over to a waiting van.

It was just as bad as the first time. Ruva's heart raced, and she whimpered with terror. The van went through crowded, noisy streets full of more humans than she dreamed possible. They passed a bus, and little humans leaned out the windows and yelled at her.

Those must be children. How horrible! she thought.

The van left the tall buildings and went along tree-lined avenues. The air became cooler. At last it went through an arch with the words DANTE'S ZOO in gloomy black letters overhead. The van eased between a gray pool full of seals and a shallow lake with flamingos standing on an island. A troop of monkeys gazed at her sadly from behind bars. The vultures in the vulture enclosure were clustered over something she couldn't quite see.

The van stopped by a cement wall with an open door. The cage was lowered. Zoo attendants stood with brooms and hoses to force Ruva to move. She remembered Rodentus's parting words and made a brave attempt to escape, but she was greatly outnumbered.

The humans turned on the fire hoses and almost

knocked her off her feet. She was swept through the door in a blast of water. She skidded along the cement until she fell against a small house at the center of the pen. The door closed.

She was alone. Really, truly alone. Behind her was a high wall and before her was an iron fence. Between was a stretch of concrete and the little house. This was where she was meant to stay for the rest of her life.

Ruva stretched out her neck and bawled as though her heart would break.

Five

FOR A WHILE, Ruva gave herself up to despair. A family of humans watched her from beyond the iron fence. "I didn't know giraffes made sounds," said one. More humans began to gather until there was a crowd of them.

"Maybe it's hungry," someone remarked. At this, everyone began to pelt Ruva with hot-dog buns, popcorn, peanuts, gum, and Popsicle sticks.

When she wouldn't eat, they tried to draw her attention to the food littering the ground. "There, giraffe. *There!* What a stupid animal! It just stepped on that gum." They shouted at her.

Then Ruva discovered the house had a door. She went inside and found a bare little room with no windows. There was enough space to lie down.

"Hey, giraffe!" the crowd yelled. "Come out.

Do something interesting." Ruva ignored them, and after a while they went away. The cool, gray dark of the room was soothing. She rested her head against a wall.

Rodentus would have been ashamed of me for crying, she thought. He hates animals who give up. Still, I put up a good fight when they drove me out of the cage. Cheered by this small victory, she began to make plans:

(1) Escape.
(2) Find a ship going to Africa.

The World is so big and confusing, she thought. Suppose I can't find Mother when I get to Africa? No, no, I mustn't lose hope. I wonder where Rodentus is now.

Ruva cried a little more at the memory of her friend, but she forced herself to take a deep breath and stop. *He* would want me to keep my spirits up, she thought.

She went out again to explore her pen. A platform by the house was loaded with hay. It was stale but filling. She drank at a cement trough. People began to gather at the fence.

"Mommy! The giraffe is looking at me!" cried a small human in its mother's arms.

"It's learning about you, just as you are learning about it," said the mother. She was more accurate than she knew. Ruva was studying people as hard as she had the nine-times table. She saw they came in different colors and sizes. Her nose twitched as it gathered information. Humans didn't all smell like dead hyenas.

The odors ranged from curious baboon to sly jackal to nervous antelope. Never had she come across a creature with such a confusing mixture of scents. It was as though all the animals had melted together. Most surprising of all, Ruva discovered humans spoke the Common Speech without realizing it!

That little girl, for example, who was trying to climb the fence, was saying, "I'm lonely!" Her mother was sighing, "I don't know what to do." Her father grumbled, "Don't bother me." And her brother simply repeated the word *hate* over and over again. They did this by standing just so and moving just so. The meaning was perfectly clear to Ruva, but none of the humans seemed to understand.

Ruva tugged at the door in the cement wall with her mouth. It was locked.

"Look! It's trying to get out," cried a boy.

"Don't be ridiculous," his father said. "It probably thinks the doorknob is something to eat. Giraffes are too stupid to think about escaping."

"That's what you think," muttered Ruva under her breath. She sampled the bushes where the fence joined the cement wall. They were bitter. She spat them out. The little giraffe measured the iron railing and decided it was too high to climb. She even tried to dig a hole in the concrete floor with her hooves.

"Just as well," she sighed. "I can't see myself crawling through a tunnel."

At the end of the day, Ruva was beginning to lose hope. All she had done was amuse the humans. She morosely chewed a cud of stale straw and watched the light fade.

A sea fog, thick and wet, rolled over Dante's Zoo. It filled the seal pond; the seals barked mournfully. It drove the monkeys, cursing, into their crowded house. It made the flamingos droop on their island. Finally, it drifted over the little giraffe.

"This is fog, I believe," she said. "Rodentus described it. Nasty, wet stuff—but excellent for escaping. At last something is working in my favor."

The fog filled the next enclosure with its clammy cold. The occupants woke up and began to complain loudly.

They were lions.

They roared in the damp darkness. A heavy odor drifted into Ruva's pen. She had never smelled it before, but every cell of her body knew what it was. *It came from the inside of a lion's mouth.* No matter that the lions were trapped as completely as she. No matter that they couldn't possibly harm her. Every cell of Ruva's body told her to flee.

She galloped around the enclosure, desperately searching for a way out. "Got—to—run," she gasped. She tried to climb the fence and fell. She threw herself against the door. Around and around she galloped until she collapsed. Her sides heaved as she struggled for breath.

[28]

The fog was so thick, she couldn't see the other end of the pen. Anything might be hiding there. *Roarrrrr!* went the lions. Ruva lay on the wet concrete and shuddered. Her brain was swamped by the inherited terror of millions of giraffes who had been hunted by lions throughout time.

After a while, the zoo became quiet. Water dripped from the trees and coated the walls of the animal houses. A gibbon howled in its sleep as it dreamed of warm forests with endless trees to swing on. Ruva lay on the concrete and stared into the darkness.

THE SUN shone weakly through the morning mist as the zoo attendants went about their work. They hosed out cages, changed water, and brought food. One of them ran for help when he discovered Ruva.

Very soon Dante, owner of the zoo, was looking her over. He was a short dark man who waved his hands and shouted when he was angry. "I paid for this animal only yesterday. Now look! You must have given her bad food."

"No, sir," said the attendant.

"So many tickets I sold. 'Come see the giraffe,' I told the visitors. 'A rare pygmy giraffe from the island of Madagascar.'"

"She's a baby, not a pygmy. She doesn't come from Madagascar," the attendant said.

"*I* know that," Dante said with a crafty smile.

"But do the customers know? They are as stupid as Thanksgiving turkeys."

"They caught on to the shaved ape you said was the missing link."

"Ah! So many tickets I sold before the news got out. Now what shall I do with this sick animal?" Dante rubbed his hands as he inspected Ruva. She caught, most distinctly, the odor of wild dog.

"Call the vet," the attendant said.

"Think of the expense!" cried Dante. He considered Ruva with his dark wild-dog eyes. "Do you suppose the museum would buy a rare Madagascan pygmy *stuffed* giraffe?"

"Hundreds of people saw her yesterday. If she dies now, the SPCA is going to ask questions." The attendant rubbed Ruva's wet fur with a towel. He didn't look up as Dante stalked away.

Six

THE VET SHOT Ruva full of antibiotics. He ran a hair dryer over her body and even gave her a spray of acacia leaves as a treat. "You get well, baby," he told her. "You don't want a sore throat with that long neck of yours." He was so kind, Ruva was tempted to explain her problem.

"Lions," she said, using the Common Speech. "I can't bear having them next door."

"Do you have fleas, baby? You keep rippling your skin and waving your ears," said the vet.

"Lions! Big! Horrible! Evil! Lions!" Ruva explained.

"Well, we'll fix that problem up. A little flea powder and hey, presto, no more nasty itches."

It was useless. The vet was completely stupid. Ruva found herself on display again as soon as he left. A crowd clustered at the fence. The shadows grew small, then large as the day dragged on. When the fog rolled in, the lions roared. Ruva lay in her house and shivered.

She quickly learned that one day of the week was worse than the rest. That was when her neighbors *weren't* fed. Their stomachs began to rumble about noon, but they weren't really uncomfortable until dark. All night they paced back and forth, roaring and talking.

"Do you remember that wild pig we caught when we were young?" one of them said.

"Oh, yes! I still have a scar from his tusks," another remembered.

"Go on! It was just a scratch. I have a much bigger one from a buffalo."

"Sheer carelessness. The whole pride was holding it down. I must be going crazy, but I smell a baby giraffe somewhere," said a lioness.

"Really? A delicious, crunchy little giraffe? *Roarrrrr!* That makes my mouth water."

It went on all night. The next day twice as many humans came to Dante's Zoo. They stood outside the lion enclosure as the beasts worked themselves into a frenzy. Finally, attendants brought meat.

"Ahhhh," sighed the crowd.

Rahhhh, howled the lions.

Then Ruva had to endure the horrid sounds of crunching from next door. She was unable to sleep or eat. This has *got* to stop, the little giraffe decided at last. What would Rodentus do? Ruva absent-mindedly tested the strength of the fence as she walked along. "If you can't run," he said, "face your enemy. Learn about him if you have time, and fight if you must." She arrived at the bushes and began to pull off the leaves.

She worked until she had removed the top branches. She was able to look across. She had never actually seen lions, although they were printed in her mind and body by ancestors. Ruva's heart pounded. She had to force herself to open her eyes—and there they were!

The great beasts sprawled around a heap of bones and buzzing flies. Some of them lay on their backs with their bellies shining in the afternoon sun. Others dozed with their chins in the water bowl as though they were too lazy to move after drinking. They were grossly fat.

Dante had discovered his biggest money-makers were the lions. People wanted to see them kill T-bone steaks, so the zoo owner fed them almost every day. Their wild cousins got to eat only once a week, or less.

The lions, simple creatures, pounced on the steaks with satisfying growls. They fought one another for bones even when their stomachs hurt from too much food. They hadn't changed much since the time of Nimrod.

Not one of them could jump the fence, Ruva thought with relief. In fact—ugh—that one can barely stand. She went back to her house and took a long nap to make up for all the sleep she had missed.

ONE DAY, Ruva was dozing in the shade of a bay laurel tree that hung over her enclosure. The tree was too high to reach, but occasional leaves drifted down. She found them delicious. A group of children had draped themselves on the fence.

"It's so boring," one of them said. "Why did we have to come the only day the lions aren't fed?"

"The teacher says it's brutal," explained a girl.

"Yeah," the other children said.

"The teacher says lions are like big cats. They play with their food and make it suffer."

"*Yeah,*" the others said with their eyes shining.

"I had a cat once." A boy tossed pebbles into Ruva's water trough. "We went to San Diego to visit Grandma, and Dad left him at her house."

"So what?" a girl said.

"My cat walked all the way home. He went along the freeways and slept on the traffic islands. He drank from the sprinklers. It took him two weeks to get home."

"Wow!"

"That's nothing," said another boy, who was trying to reach Ruva with a long strand of grass. "We went to Washington, D.C., and lost our cat at the Washington Monument. He hopped a freight train to Saint Louis, walked across the Great Plains, and climbed the Rocky Mountains. On the way he ate prairie dogs. It took him two months to get home."

"Neat!" the other children said.

"You think that's great?" A girl with many tight little braids swung from the top bar of the fence. Ruva thought the braids looked like acacia thorns.

"We lost our cat in Patagonia, at the tip of South America," said the girl. "She caught a boat through the Panama Canal and walked up the coast of Mexico. She ate baby sharks out of tide pools. When she got to the border, she swam the Colorado River, caught a Greyhound bus, and got off right outside our door. It took her a *whole year*, and when she arrived, she had a litter of Patagonian kittens."

Nobody said anything for a while. Nobody could top that story.

"If we can get the teacher to stay till four, I hear they feed the boa constrictor a chicken," a boy finally said. This cheered everyone up. The children began to drift away. Someone asked the girl with the braids what Patagonian kittens were like.

"They're horrible. Their fur sticks out like iron filings," she replied.

After they were gone, Ruva thought and thought. People sure lose a lot of cats, she decided. Rodentus taught me all about oceans and continents, but I have no idea what to do when I reach Africa. I'll ask a cat how to find home.

There was only one cat at the zoo. It was a scrawny female with a nest of kittens near the duck pond. Ruva had noticed her because the mother cat did a wonderful thing. *She climbed into the lion cage and stole their meat.* She waited until they were gorged and sleeping on their backs, but still it took tremendous courage. Ruva was awed by her.

"Excuse me. May I ask you a question?" the little giraffe called as the animal groomed herself under a bush.

The cat, like all cats, was curious. She listened politely to Ruva's tale and thought for a long time. "It's not anything I *do*," she said at last. "I simply *know* where home is."

"Can't you tell me anything?"

The mother cat thought some more. "If I turn around like this, I can feel where my kittens are. It's like a Warm Place in the air. When they turn around, they know where *I* am, too."

Ruva waited as the cat licked her paw and tidied her ears. "Your body is wise," she said at last. "It knows when you are tired or sleepy. It knows a great many other things, too. If you are very quiet, it will tell you where home is."

She trotted off as a zoo attendant came along the walk.

That night, Ruva came out of her house and stood in the fog. It was cold, and, for once, even the lions were quiet. A chill dew coated the little house and made the concrete floor icy. Water dripped off the bay laurel tree.

Ruva turned and waited and turned again. I mustn't reason it out, she thought. Rodentus taught me about logic, and that's one kind of thinking. I believe this is different.

She let her mind become quiet, almost asleep, as she turned. And then she felt it. Far, far away, like a little patch of sun on a winter day, something wavered in the mist. Ruva took a deep breath and turned again. Yes, there it was! Out there, beyond the fog and ocean, was a Warm Place that belonged to her and her alone. It was home.

Ruva was so happy, she galloped around the pen. "Settle down!" yelled one of the lions from next door. "Can't we get any peace around here?" Ruva banged her hooves on the cement and galloped again.

The next day everything looked different. The sky was bluer, the trees greener; even the children were almost attractive. "I know where home is now," Ruva said, hugging the secret close. "All I have to do is escape."

Seven

ALL SHE HAD to do was escape!
She couldn't climb, she couldn't bur-
row, she couldn't fly. To make things
worse, people didn't stop by her enclosure as often.

At first, Ruva hated the visits. Now she knew
her life depended on them. Animals who didn't sell
tickets disappeared. First to go was the shaved ape
Dante tried to pass off as the missing link. Then an
elderly coyote who refused to howl went missing.
Ruva heard about them from the sea gulls who
rested on their way to the seal pond.

The zoo visitors had found out there weren't
any giraffes at all—pygmy or otherwise—in Madagascar. It had been in the newspaper. Ruva had no
tricks to entertain them. She didn't balance a ball
on her nose like the seals or kill T-bones like the

lions. She just stood there being a giraffe, and that wasn't enough.

"Has the museum read the paper?" asked Dante, watching Ruva with his wild-dog eyes.

"Everyone has read the paper," the attendant said. "They won't buy a phony rare Madagascan pygmy stuffed giraffe."

"Pity," said Dante.

She had to escape soon, but she hadn't the slightest idea how to do it. One day a pair of children—the only ones for hours—stood by the fence and popped their gum. "Boring old giraffe," said the girl.

"I wish I had a peashooter. I'd wake it up," the boy said. "How's that African chameleon?"

Chameleon? thought Ruva.

"Dead, I think. I tried to feed it gum, but it wouldn't open its mouth. Its eyes are closed."

"Yep, that's a dead chameleon all right," said the boy. "Throw it away and let's go spit on the crocodiles."

Something was tossed through the bars. The children moved off. Ruva cautiously approached the thing and sniffed it. She had to straddle the ground to get her head down far enough.

"Hold it, sweetheart! One inch closer and I make macramé out of that nose."

Ruva jumped. "You're alive!"

"Bet your booties. Are those creeps gone?" The chameleon opened one eye and swiveled it at the fence.

"Everyone's gone. Tell me, are you an *African* chameleon?"

"Are you an *African* giraffe?" the lizard said rudely. "What else would I be?"

"I'm sorry," said Ruva. "You're smaller than the ones I remember."

"You'd be small, too, if you were owned by a pair of hairless apes who think bubble gum is health food."

"Is there anything I can do?" The giraffe gazed with delight at the lizard. His toes splayed out on the concrete, and his buggy eyes pointed in opposite directions. He could have come straight from the grassland where Ruva was born.

"Just point me at the nearest bug. And watch those big feet of yours." The chameleon walked to a position under the food platform. Dante sometimes supplied Ruva with old vegetables from a market. Bits fell to the ground and were too difficult to reach.

The chameleon sat perfectly still until a fly landed near one of these. Then *zap*! Out came his strange jointed tongue and snatched it up with the clasper at the end. It looked like a little arm shooting out of his mouth.

Ruva waited politely until the creature had satisfied his hunger. "Ahh! That felt good. Now I need to sleep. Where's the safest spot?"

"My house," Ruva replied. "Only, the attendant sometimes looks inside."

"Don't worry about that, sweetheart. Hiding is what I do best. Just *you* remember where I am, or I might have to get nasty."

The chameleon placed himself in the darkest part of the room. The wall was gray and streaked with mold. As Ruva watched, the lizard seemed to fade away. His skin turned gray and blotchy until he was only a faint shadow.

"That's wonderful," sighed the little giraffe.

"Take a hike," the chameleon said. "No offense, but I'm planning some serious nap time. Those creeps watched television until after midnight."

Ruva tiptoed away. She stood against the fence and paid no attention to the humans passing by. Her heart felt as light as the clouds drifting along in the blue sky. She had a friend again.

THE chameleon's name was Nelson. He swaggered around the enclosure and even went to look at the lions. "More flies over there, you know," he told Ruva.

"Aren't you afraid of them?"

"*They're* afraid of *me*. Nothing freezes a lion's gizzard more than the sight of an angry chameleon. It's built-in, like how elephants run from mice and humans freak out if a spider drops on them. Watch."

Nelson went next door. Ruva peered over the bushes. The lizard turned himself purple and bugged out his eyes. "You! Lions!" he yelled. "I'm coming for lunch. Stay out of my way or I'll put a spell on you!"

"Yes, sir. Yes, sir," cried the lions, crowding into a heap against the far wall. "Don't look at us with those buggy eyes! Don't put a spell on us!"

Nelson sat by the meat bones until his stomach bulged with flies. "Don't move or I'll turn you all into slimy earthworms!" he threatened as he returned to Ruva's enclosure. The lions moaned with terror.

"Wonderful to get decent food again," he said as he perched on the edge of Ruva's water trough. "Of course, flies can get boring after a while. What I would really, *really* like is a tasty African mole cricket. Ah, mole crickets," he sighed as he adjusted his color to match the trough. "They used to come out of their holes after the rains. Boy, I can still taste them."

"I'm not a boy. I'm a girl," Ruva said gently.

"Who can tell with giraffes? Remember how the rains used to sweep across the grass, and how the air filled with flying termites? They were okay, too. I wish I could go home."

"Me, too," said Ruva.

"But we don't know the way." Nelson's skin lost some of its color.

"I know the way."

The chameleon swiveled both his eyes to study the little giraffe.

"I really do," insisted Ruva. "A cat told me.

You turn around and around until you can feel a Warm Place far away. That's home."

"Hmm," the chameleon said. He climbed down from the trough and turned around and around. "I feel like a dumb dog getting ready to sleep. Nope, I don't feel a thing."

"Maybe that's because you're cold-blooded. I mean that kindly," Ruva added as Nelson began to turn purple. "Rodentus told me about it. He was a dear friend of mine, but I lost him." She swallowed bravely. "Warm-blooded animals—like me—make their own heat. Cold-blooded ones get it from outside."

"That's right. I have to sit in the sun every morning," the lizard agreed.

"Well, the cat said she could feel where her kittens were, and they could feel her. Maybe I'm sending out a warm message at the same time Mother is sending it back." At the thought of Mother, Ruva was so overcome with sadness she couldn't go on.

"*My* mother wouldn't know me from a mushroom," Nelson said. "She laid the eggs and took off without a backward glance."

"I'm sorry," said Ruva.

"It's how we chameleons are. You know, we ought to escape together. You can tell me the way, and I can travel on your back to protect you."

Ruva gazed into the distance. She saw the humans pass by on the walk. She saw the roof of a hot-dog stand, some dark green Dumpsters, and the side of a monkey cage across the way. Afternoon clouds were beginning to lower and turn into fog. A flock of swallows swirled out of the mist and up again.

Swallows! They went to and from Africa every year. If such little birds could travel such great distances . . .

"We can do it," Ruva said, "if you open the door."

Eight

I AM NOT A MONKEY," Nelson said crossly.
"You're much more clever," Ruva coaxed.
"Poke the tip of your tail into the keyhole
and—what did Rodentus call it?—pick the lock."

"Who is this Rodentus you keep talking about?"

"He taught me about the World when I was
captured. He's a wonderful friend! Intelligent,
loyal—"

"Why don't you ask *him* for help? I'm just a
stupid old lizard." Nelson clamped his mouth shut
in a stubborn line.

"Because you're wonderful, too. You can hide
anywhere, and you're not afraid of lions. I'm lucky
to have such good friends." Ruva lowered her head,
on which the chameleon perched. Muttering under

his breath, Nelson climbed onto the doorknob. He clung to it with his toes.

"This Rodentus, is he a chameleon?"

"He's a rat—"

"That explains it!" cried Nelson. "He's a thieving garbage eater. No wonder he knows how to pick locks."

"Rodentus has dined with kings and presidents," Ruva said.

"Oh, sure! The same way a roach has lunch in a restaurant."

"Please try," she urged.

The lizard uncurled his tail and fished inside the keyhole. "Why do creatures always hand me the tough jobs? 'Oh, Nelson, just balance on this cliff,' they say. Females are the worst— Help! Ow!" The door swung open, and the chameleon was thrown against the wall.

"Bring the hose," Dante called to his assistant. Ruva scampered away from the jet of water. She could see Nelson lying in a puddle. He was the color of wet cement.

"All you do is eat up my profits," said Dante, kicking at the little giraffe. He dumped hay onto the platform. The assistant sprayed a stream of water to clean the floor. Nelson slid along in the current and landed against the bushes. "Do you think I could make a coat out of her?" asked the zookeeper.

"The SPCA would make you a whole lawsuit," the assistant replied.

Dante slammed the door on the way out.

Ruva immediately went to Nelson and nudged him.

"Don't *ever* ask me to do that again," the chameleon hissed. "Look at my tail!"

Ruva saw with horror that the tip of it was broken off. "Does—does it hurt?"

"*Does it hurt?* No, it feels wonderful, you stupid giraffe! I don't know why I didn't do it before. I think I'll get my toes chopped off next." Nelson curled his tail, tucking the injured part into the middle. He spent the rest of the morning brooding by the trough. Ruva was afraid he would leave without her.

In the afternoon, he visited the lions. Ruva heard them cry, "We'll be good! Don't look at us!" The lizard came back in a good mood. He swaggered across the enclosure and only winced slightly when he used his tail to climb the food platform.

"I've been thinking," he announced. "How will you hide if we get out of here?"

Ruva was relieved to hear him say *we* and not *I*. He must have forgiven her. "I hadn't thought about it," she said.

"You stick out like a buffalo in a bathtub. I wish you knew how to change color."

"I could learn," said Ruva.

"I'm not sure how to teach you." The chameleon moved to one side as Ruva fed on the hay. He swiveled his eyes in opposite directions.

"Doesn't that give you a headache?" Ruva asked.

[47]

"Feels great. Now listen. All I know is that when I stand next to a wall, I feel *wall* inside. After a while, I *am* wall."

"What happens with the lions?"

"Ah! That's special. Lions make me feel a hundred feet tall with fangs that drip acid and claws that rip up railroad tracks!"

"Goodness!" Ruva cried.

Nelson had turned bright purple before her eyes. His eyes bugged out like big purple grapes. He hissed loudly as though letting off steam. Then, gradually, his color faded until it was the mottled yellow-brown of the hay. "Well, you see what lions do to me," he said.

"Can you teach me *that*?" breathed Ruva.

"No, I can't. I don't understand it myself." Nelson climbed down to nap in the shade of the little house.

Ruva stood by the wall and thought, Make me gray. Make me hard. She tried to imagine *wall* inside. A group of humans waved cotton candy at her from the fence.

She stood by the bushes and thought, Make me green. Make me leafy. She worked on changing color until she saw spots before her eyes.

"Do you have a stomachache?" remarked Nelson.

"Can you see me?"

"Heck, yes. You look terrible."

Ruva went back to her house. She intended to

rest only a few moments, but trying to change color had exhausted her. She fell sound asleep.

The grassland lay around her with its clusters of trees. She was very small. The World was still only one day's walk in that direction and one day's walk in this direction. Her aunts and uncles moved in stately groups as they browsed. One minute she could see them quite clearly; the next minute all that was visible was a grove of trees.

"What happened?" asked Ruva in that faraway grassland.

"That is Giraffe Magic. You will learn it when you're older," Mother said.

Ruva woke with a jerk. "Giraffe Magic! And there was Buffalo Magic and Hippo Magic and much, much more. I can do it if I find the key. It's like the Warm Place, waiting for me to discover it."

She went out to the bushes and looked at her next-door neighbors. The big cats were sprawled untidily in the remains of a meal. *Lion*, she thought. Thousands of ancestral giraffes answered in her body.

Hide, they said. *Become tree. Become shadow. Become wind.*

She heard the thudding of hooves and smelled the red dust. She felt a hot, heavy breath on her neck. Ruva's heart beat rapidly, and she panted for air. She no longer tried to be something else; she *was* something else.

One of the lions glanced up and said, "I don't

remember that tree. They must be remodeling next door."

"Who cares?" said another lion. "Pass me that femur. I'm feeling quite hollow inside."

The little giraffe stepped back with a thrill of triumph. I did it! she thought. But, oh, my head aches! How does anyone do this for more than a minute?

Nine

AY AFTER DAY, she practiced. She stood in front of the few humans who visited her enclosure and willed herself to *disappear*. The adults soon scratched their heads and said, "The sign says Giraffe. Why can't we see anything?"

"There it is!" cried the children. They were much more difficult to fool.

Nelson quickly tired of the game. He set off on long expeditions around the zoo. "Might as well find an escape route," he explained. He discovered a group of lonely female lizards in the reptile house and spent his afternoons there.

On the day Ruva vanished before an entire class of third graders, she told Nelson she was ready to go.

"I'm ready, too," he said. "The Gila monster's talking about marriage."

"Could you, *would* you, dear Nelson, climb onto the doorknob and pick the lock again?"

The chameleon groaned. "Why does every female expect me to run errands? 'Oh, Nelson, bring me a moth. Nelson, scratch my back—I'm molting.' The answer is no! You got half my tail. You're not getting the rest of it."

Ruva was about to argue when she saw Dante coming along the walk with two attendants.

"This is the house I want carted away," the zookeeper said, stopping in front of the enclosure.

"Shall we do it now?" asked one of the attendants.

"Tomorrow's okay. The hyenas don't arrive till morning." The men strode off.

"Tomorrow?" whispered Ruva.

"I'd like to put a spell on that rotten brute!" Nelson was beginning to turn purple. "Don't worry, sweetheart. I know this zoo forward and backward. I'll find you."

"Nelson . . . they didn't say anything about moving me."

"You can't mean—" The chameleon turned almost white with shock.

The two were silent for a long time. The third graders came back and yelled at the little giraffe. She barely heard them.

"Dante has probably sold me to another zoo. You mustn't worry," said Ruva.

"Oh, stop it!" Nelson cried. "I hate it when females say, 'Don't worry.' They mean just the opposite. 'Let's ask good old Nelson to rescue us,' they say. '*He* won't mind donating a tail to the cause.' " He grumbled as he stumped across the enclosure. "I'll be back late," he called as he slipped under the fence.

Ruva spent an anxious afternoon and evening. She trotted up and down from sheer nerves. What can I do? she thought. I can't get out. Where's Nelson? Oh, what shall I do? She was ready to throw herself against the bars when, at about midnight, two figures crept under the fence.

"Nelson!" cried the little giraffe. "And—is that *Rodentus?*"

"No, miss," said the rat, bowing. "The name's Troll. I am a guest of Mr. Dante."

"Guest, hah!" Nelson snorted.

Now that the rat was close, Ruva saw he was nothing like Rodentus. His fur was scarred and his muzzle gray. Troll scratched his belly with long dirty fingernails.

"I am pleased to make your acquaintance," the little giraffe said.

"Likewise. The lizard says you got a job for me," said Troll.

"I found him in the reptile house, stealing the attendant's lunch," Nelson said. Ruva was afraid Troll would take offense, but he seemed flattered.

She wasn't sure how to put it politely. "A dear friend told me that all rats are natural lock pickers—"

"And thieves," added Nelson.

"I need to escape right away, so if you wouldn't mind—"

"Escape!" The rat laughed harshly. "A baby like you wouldn't last ten seconds in the real World."

"That's our business!" growled the chameleon.

"So it is. Well, I don't mind turning a profit. What have you got to offer?"

"You didn't say anything about pay," Nelson shouted.

"Only a noodlehead would do a job for free."

"Only a lying rat would ask a *baby* to pay!" The chameleon's eyes began to bug out.

"Liar? Me? I don't sweet-talk innocent Gila monsters!"

"Please!" Ruva cried. "Rodentus told me humans use pieces of green paper called money. Is that what you want?"

Troll laughed so hard the tears ran down his face. He had to wipe them with the tip of his scabby tail. "Dante keeps his money in a big black suitcase. He doesn't trust banks. I chewed my way in there three months ago." He was overcome with a fit of giggles and couldn't go on.

"You made a nest?" Nelson gazed at the rat with slightly more respect.

"You have no idea how comfortable one hundred thousand dollars of shredded green paper can be. I don't need that kind of money, kid. Rats deal in scuttlebutt. You give me information. I trade it for favors down the line. For example, who is this Rodentus you mention?"

Ruva proceeded to explain how she met her friend and how he was on a secret mission. As she spoke, Troll became more and more excited. He chittered softly and wrung his grimy paws.

Finally, he couldn't stand it anymore. "That's the best news I've ever had!" he cried. "You are three-times lucky to have run into him. I thought it was just any Rodentus—it's a common name— but *Rodentus von Stroheim the Third*! Oh my! Wait'll I tell the boys back at the dump!"

"He's only a rat," Nelson said coldly.

"He's the Tawny Prince, the slyest, boldest, and baddest of us all. He's what it means to be a Perfect Rat."

"Ugh," said Nelson.

"Of *course* I'll help you, Miss Ruva. Lift me to the lock, and I'll have it open in a jiffy."

The little giraffe lowered her head until Troll was able to leap aboard. He scrambled between her horns to the doorknob, inserted his tail, and *click*! The door was unlocked. "I felt a bit of old gristle inside," he said.

"Don't tell me!" Nelson winced.

Ruva took the doorknob in her teeth and pulled. The three of them, rat, lizard, and giraffe, stared out at the dark road behind the pens. Everything was silent except for the fog dripping off the bay laurel tree and the whistling snore of a lion.

"I'm *free*," Ruva whispered.

Ten

SHE WAS A SWIRL in a mist and a ripple in a stream. On her back rode a ghostly lizard and at her feet scampered the shadow of a rat. From far away, beyond the fog and ocean, a patch of sunlight stole into the dreams of the zoo.

It touched the monkeys, who muttered with uneasy dreams. It passed the vultures wheeling in remembered skies. It floated over the pond. The sound of the open sea made the seals groan as they slept.

The warmth spread in ever-widening rings until it fetched up against the trailer where Dante slept. He was a boy again, lying on a green hillside and looking up at a rainbow. "Home," whispered the zookeeper in his sleep. Then the ring passed on. Dante, still asleep, felt under his bed for the suitcase where he kept his money.

Be mist, be tree, whispered thousands of giraffe ancestors as Ruva walked silently toward the zoo gate.

Be grass, be stone, said thousands of chameleons to the fleeing Nelson.

Where's the cheese? asked thousands of shadow rats.

Ruva, Nelson, and Troll came to the gate. It was locked, and the spell was broken.

"Can you open it, Troll?" Nelson asked.

"Look at the size of that padlock. My tail isn't made out of steel." The rat slumped—no longer invisible—by the road.

"Don't look at me," said Nelson.

The little giraffe shook her head to rid it of the voices of her ancestors. "Is this all? Is this as far as I get?"

"Of course not," said Troll. "The Tawny Prince would never forgive us if we gave up this easily. I know a perfect hiding place on the flamingo island. You can wait until the gate opens."

"You mean *disappear* in broad daylight? With everyone watching?" Ruva's heart began to pound.

"Unless you have a better idea."

"You did it in daylight before," said Nelson.

"That was different! It didn't matter if I failed! I *can't* do it long enough to walk out—and find a place to hide—" She was getting dangerously close to crying.

"Listen, sweetheart." The chameleon climbed the little giraffe's neck until he was perched between her horns. "Your relatives hide from lions every day. Do you think they whine about the amount of sunlight?"

So Ruva, with Nelson on her head and Troll on her back, waded across the pond to a reed-covered island. She found the flamingos asleep, each with its head under one wing. The other wing was clipped to keep them from flying away.

"You see?" the rat said. "No one will see you among all these leggy birds. The attendant only cleans up once a week."

"You sound like you come here a lot," remarked Nelson.

"Flamingos lay delicious eggs."

"You're disgusting," the chameleon said.

WHEN DAWN CAME, the birds were outraged to find intruders. They withdrew in a noisy cluster to the opposite end of the island. Attendants went to and fro in the zoo, cleaning cages, watering plants, and carting food to the animals. At any moment someone would notice Ruva was missing. The flamingos flapped their wings and shrieked, "Enemies!" but no one paid any attention.

"For once I'm glad humans don't know the Common Speech," Ruva said.

"Look!" said Nelson. "They're opening the gate."

Hordes of schoolchildren flocked in. They shouted and screamed as they jostled past the ticket stand. Soon they were everywhere. They threw rocks into the flamingo pond until Dante threatened to feed them to the grizzly bear.

"I can't go out in that," Ruva cried.

"You have to," said Nelson.

"Come on, Miss Ruva. Think of the triumph if you walked out under their noses." Troll leaned over her shoulder and tickled her neck with his vibrissae.

"Leave me alone!" she bleated.

A large van honked as it rolled in the front gate. The children jumped up and down to see what was inside. Something threw itself against the back window with a vicious snarl.

"*Hyenas,*" gasped Ruva.

She watched the van nose along the road toward her enclosure. A moment later, someone cried, "The giraffe's missing!"

"Lock the gates!" Dante shouted.

"Escaped wild animal!" shrilled the children, beside themselves with joy. "We'll hunt it down! We'll find it!"

Nelson groaned and Troll's teeth chattered. The van came back and stopped before the locked gate. "Open up! I've got a schedule to keep," yelled the driver.

"I've lost my beautiful giraffe," Dante cried. "Pearl of the zoo and darling of my heart!"

"Liar," muttered Nelson.

"Ask me if I care, you skinflint. Open that gate!" the driver said.

They were standing directly in front of the flamingo pond.

"How do I know," Dante said sweetly, "that you didn't help yourself to a giraffe when no one was watching? I want to see inside that van."

"You and who else, buddy!" The driver leaned on his horn. Troll put his paws to his ears.

"I don't *need* anyone else," snarled Dante, yanking open the back door. The driver jumped out of the van and swung at the zookeeper. Dante moved remarkably fast. He darted in and out with a blow that landed on the driver's nose.

"Good footwork," remarked Troll.

"But bad strategy," Nelson said.

The driver lunged. He lifted Dante right off the ground and hurled him into the flamingo pond. The zookeeper floundered in a mess of dirty water and feathers, screaming insults. The other man staggered to a water fountain to rinse his bloody face. Attendants ran forward to open the gate. Not one of them lifted a finger to help Dante.

From the moment the quarrel began, something strange happened inside Ruva's head. The weariness and fear faded away. Hundreds of other giraffes seemed to be standing behind her. She turned to look, and they melted into the reeds. *Listen*, said the giraffe ancestors in her mind. And then: *Now!*

She began walking through the pond. Nelson and Troll crouched on her back. *Be water, be wind*, chanted the giraffe ancestors as Ruva made her dreamlike passage through the water.

She moved directly in front of Dante. She walked through a cluster of children who were jeering at the zookeeper from the shore. The gate was before her, but the whispered voices in her mind grew dim. She knew she could never reach it. She turned abruptly and climbed through the open door of the van.

The driver, wiping his face with a handkerchief, slammed it shut.

Ruva slumped against the side, more tired than she had ever been in her life. Nelson clamped his toes onto her back as the van roared off.

"Never, never have I seen a finer trick," sighed Troll.

"What are you doing here? Isn't the zoo your home?" Nelson said rudely.

"A rat's home is what's directly under his feet. I just have to see what happens next. Oh, the artistry of it! The supreme beauty of ripping off Dante in front of his face!"

"Be quiet. She's sick," snapped the chameleon.

Ruva felt as though she was going to faint. Her head ached and her mouth was bitter. *Disappearing* was far more demanding than running at top speed. She couldn't possibly do it for more than a few minutes. The metal side of the van bumped her head painfully. She was too weak to do anything about it. The reek of hyenas surrounded her as though the evil creatures were still present. Nelson and Troll watched her anxiously as the van jolted through the city streets.

Eleven

RUVA HAD RECOVERED by the time the van jerked to a stop. The driver got out. "You're late!" someone called.

"I had to squeeze every nickel out of Dante. I hope the rats eat his money," the driver answered.

Troll stuffed his tail into his mouth to stifle his giggles.

The human voices died away. Ruva, Nelson, and Troll listened to the hum of engines, tinkle of metal, and slap of water against wood. "I believe this is the harbor," the rat said.

"How would you know?" said Nelson.

"Every rat worth his salt ships out at least once in his life. I was sailing before Miss Ruva was born."

"What kind of ships?" The lizard climbed

Ruva's neck until he could see out the window in the back door.

"Pirate ships."

"It figures. Ruva, sweetheart. Could you work the handle of the door?"

The little giraffe turned it with her mouth. Troll poked his nose through the opening. "Ah! That's fine. That's sea air." He took a deep breath.

"See if it's safe," said Nelson.

The rat streaked to the edge of the dock and looked around. "All clear," he called. Ruva cautiously stepped out with Nelson clinging to her horns. Dozens of sea gulls strolled along the boardwalk and exchanged friendly insults.

"Disappear," whispered Nelson from Ruva's head.

"I'm too tired!"

"Do it. There's a sailor on that coil of rope."

The little giraffe tried, but her ancestors remained distant and silent. There was nothing she could do but walk boldly past the human. He stared at her. His eyes got wider and wider.

"Son of a gun," he whispered, looking at the bottle of rum in his hand. "I see a *giraffe*—with a *lizard* on its head—and a *rat* running at its heels. That does it! No more booze for me!" He flung the bottle into the water and staggered off as fast as he could.

Small sailing craft were moored, side by side, along the dock. Their masts were decorated with pieces of tin that jingled in the breeze. Some of the boats were battered fishing vessels, some were family runabouts, and a few were long, squat houseboats with potted plants on the roof.

At the end of the dock, where the water was deepest, was the grandest of them all: a magnificent yacht with a sweeping prow and a wide expanse of window. Its hull was dazzling white, and the natural wood trim had been polished until it shone like a brown jewel.

"Now *that's* a boat," the rat said reverently.

"We have to hide," Ruva murmured. Her legs were beginning to get wobbly.

"Excuse me, my good bird." The chameleon halted a passing sea gull. "Are any of these ships going to Africa?"

"Hoo! You mangy barnacle with legs!" it squawked.

"You squishy sponge covered with rotten seaweed," cried Troll before Nelson could turn purple. "Insults are considered good manners among sea gulls," he whispered. "They show you're a regular guy."

"I don't suppose a clam brain like you would know which of these boats is off to Africa," the rat continued.

"Course I know, you stepped-on old squid face." The bird indicated the shining yacht at the end of the dock. "The *Apocalypso*'s on its way tonight. Came in this morning with a load of hyenas."

Ruva swayed on her hooves as she crossed the

gangplank. "I can imagine easier creatures to smuggle than giraffes," Nelson grumbled as he clamped his toes onto her fur.

"That's half the sport," said Troll, scampering ahead. "Anybody can hide diamonds, but a giraffe? It's a trick worthy of the Tawny Prince."

"He's only another rat," Nelson said crossly.

The yacht was even more magnificent close up. They passed a dining room set with china and silver. A chandelier glittered overhead, and crystal pitchers shone on spotless white tablecloths.

"Wowie! This place is loaded with grub!" Troll raced to a table. It was protected by a gauze tent, but it only took the rat a second to wriggle underneath. He dived into a bowl of caviar resting in a bed of ice.

"My life's dream is complete! Oh, ecstasy! To lie on chilled caviar on a hot day!"

"Get out of there, you stupid creature!" Nelson yelled.

"Cream puffs!" shrieked Troll. He burrowed into one end of the pastry and came out the other, covered with white foam.

"Someone's coming!"

The rat slithered off the table and streaked out the door just as someone came in from the kitchen.

"Well, that was just fine," Nelson muttered. "What do you do for an encore? Set off a fire alarm?" Ruva tottered down a hallway, and Troll trotted beside her. His paws left fishy footprints on the spotless floor.

"The doors are locked," whimpered the little giraffe. She wrenched at the handles with her mouth.

"Don't lose hope. Ah! I believe that's an elevator. This *is* a fancy yacht. Just press the button with your nose, Miss Ruva."

She obeyed. "Inside!" ordered the rat as the door slid open. He climbed nimbly to her back and leaned out to press the down button. Ruva had never seen an elevator. When the floor dropped out from under her, she screamed. "Boagh! We're falling!"

"Shut up!" cried Nelson. Ruva threw herself against the wall. Troll fell off and darted here and there to escape her hooves. The chameleon wrapped his tail around her horns and hung on grimly. The elevator door opened. Ruva galloped out, bleating with fear.

"This way!" shouted Troll. He nipped the little giraffe on the ankle to get her attention. Panting with terror, she followed him into a dimly lighted little room. She tripped over a bundle of clothing and sprawled against a large spool attached to a heavy chain.

Troll caught the edge of the door with his teeth and dragged it shut. Then all three animals sat in the half dark to catch their breath.

"You stink of fish," Nelson said at last.

"Isn't it lovely?" agreed the rat. "This has been the most exciting, wonderful day of my life! First, I smuggle an *entire giraffe* out from under Dante's nose. Then I lie on a bed of chilled caviar and bathe in the innards of a cream puff. My friends, it doesn't get any better than this!"

"It—it really *is* a giraffe," came a halting voice from the bundle of clothing Ruva had tripped over.

All three animals froze as the clothing sat up and turned into a human child.

Twelve

I T WAS ALL FOR NOTHING," Ruva said in a heartbroken voice. She leaned against the wall, too tired to stand anymore. Nelson had his mouth open. Troll's hackles were up. His eyes gleamed redly. "The way I learned to find home, the *disappearing* exercises, the escape—all for nothing. I might as well swim to Africa for all the good it will do me."

"You don't have to swim," said the boy. "This boat is going there anyway."

For a moment, none of the animals realized what had happened. Then Nelson said, "I must be nuts. I could have sworn that human spoke to us."

"I did." The boy sat up, and they saw that the bundle of clothes was really a tattered sleeping bag.

"It was a lucky guess," said Troll. "Humans are

always trying to talk to animals. 'Come here, my little woogie-wums. Come and get your kitty snacks.' That sort of thing."

"I *did* talk. I would never say anything as dumb as 'woogie-wums,' " the boy insisted.

"Remarkable," said Troll. "You could almost train it to sit up and beg."

"Wait!" Ruva bent forward to sniff him. "He doesn't smell like a human. Mother said they stank like dead hyenas, but at the zoo they could be almost anything. Dante was like a wild dog."

"You're telling me," said Nelson.

"This one is different. He's . . . nice."

"Thank you." The boy laughed. "Nobody ever told me I smelled nice before, especially on this ship."

"Rodentus—wait, it's coming back to me!" Ruva felt her heart race with hope. "Rodentus said that a few humans understood the Common Speech!"

"He told me that, too," said the boy. "I've always known how, but people said I was crazy— other humans, I mean. He said it was a rare gift."

"Did—you say—*he*?" Ruva stammered.

"Sure. Rodentus von Stroheim the Third. Without him, I would have died long ago. He's training me to escape when the time comes."

"You know the Tawny Prince?" chittered Troll.

"My friend and teacher?" cried Ruva.

"Another lousy rat," Nelson muttered.

All the animals started talking at once. Ruva

was beside herself with joy. "It's worked out perfectly. I'm going home! Mother will be so happy."

"I can't believe I'm going to meet *him*," babbled the rat. "Wait'll I tell him I smuggled a whole giraffe!"

"Hold it!" Nelson said. "This human has been talking about *escape*. Does this look like a hotel room?"

Ruva studied the dim gray walls. The metal floor was coated with dirty grease. Half the space was taken up by a giant spool of chain, which fed into a hole. Water sloshed not far away.

"It . . . isn't fancy," she said.

"Wake up, sweetheart. This is a prison."

"He's right." The boy crawled out of the sleeping bag, and they saw that his neck was ringed by a metal collar. A chain went from it to a bolt in the wall. "I'm a slave," he said.

M Y NAME is Jabila. I used to live in San Francisco," the boy explained. "After school, I used to climb a hill and look at the Golden Gate Bridge. Big ships went in and out all the time. I said to myself, They're going somewhere *wonderful*. They're going to Africa.

"Africa is where my ancestors come from, you see. At school, the teacher talked a lot about finding our roots. I thought, Someday I'm going to look for my roots. I'll bet my great-great-great-grandfather was a king. That's the kind of nonsense I believed then. My great-great-great-grandfather was probably a starving peasant."

"You don't know that," Troll said kindly.

"It doesn't matter now." Jabila felt the metal collar, and the corners of his mouth turned down. "I was such a fool."

"What happened next?" said Ruva.

"I never fit in. For one thing, I could talk to animals. They sent me to the school psychiatrist so I quickly learned to lie about it. Then I looked around at my mother's apartment, and it seemed so *ugly*. It was dark. All the furniture was worn out. I was ashamed of it, and I was ashamed of Mother.

"She was worn out, too. She dressed in second-hand clothes. Her shoes had holes in them. I hated it when she picked me up at school. We didn't have a car. She walked all the way from work and walked me home. She looked so awful compared to the other mothers!"

"Sounds like you were a poisonous little brat," remarked Nelson.

"I was," the boy said in a mournful voice. "I told the other kids she was the housekeeper. I said my real mother was a famous lawyer. One day, Mom visited the classroom."

"Uh-oh," said Troll.

"She told everyone how proud she was of me, and I—I said she was lying. She wasn't my mother!

I can still see her face." Jabila buried his head in his arms and wept bitterly. Ruva nuzzled him. Troll crept onto his lap and leaned against the boy's chest.

"We've all told a lie or two in our time," whispered the rat. "You were very young."

"Mothers are very forgiving," added Ruva.

"Do you think so? That's what Rodentus said." Jabila wiped his eyes on his grimy sleeve. "I ran out of school and caught a bus down to the docks. I stowed away on the richest, most beautiful yacht I could find. And here I am."

An engine started up nearby. It vibrated the walls, and the boat began to shudder in the water. "We're leaving!" cried Nelson. "Quick, Troll! You have to go."

"A rat's home is what lies directly under his feet. Besides, Dante's bound to find out what happened to his money. Then it's *zzzt* for me!" The rat drew his paw across his throat.

Shouts came from the deck. Ropes slithered, and the anchor began to rise. Chain began to feed onto the spool, rattling out of the hole in the floor and spilling oily water everywhere. "Ugh!" said Ruva, scrambling to her feet.

The spool turned with a thundering roar until the anchor clanged into a chamber in the hull of the boat. The room was now half-filled with chain. There was barely room for Jabila and the animals.

"They'll come for me once we're away from shore," the boy said. The engine ground and whined as the yacht backed out of the harbor. Finally, it settled into a more bearable hum.

The door slammed open. Ruva crammed herself into the narrow space between the anchor chain and the wall. The top of her head stuck out in the shadows.

A man unlocked Jabila's neck ring and kicked him through the door. "Bath first, you miserable dirt bag. You'd put a vulture off his lunch."

Ruva thought her heart would jump out of her chest. For an instant the man's face turned toward her before he stomped out the door after the unhappy boy. It was Captain Skeekee!

Thirteen

THE SEA ROLLED AWAY on either side of the yacht as it steamed through the waters. Ruva woke with a raging thirst. She was alarmed by the engine noise until she remembered where she was.

"Nelson?" she called.

He was panting with the heat. Troll was nowhere in sight. Ruva pushed the door open, and the lizard scuttled out of the anchor room. He didn't speak until he had found a puddle of water and squatted in it. "That's better," he sighed. "You've been asleep for hours."

Ruva sniffed the water: it was oily and brackish. She thought longingly of the crystal pitchers upstairs. She nosed along the walls of the ship's hold until she found a leaky pipe. She licked it until her throat stopped aching, but she was still thirsty.

"I wonder how long it takes to get to Africa," she said.

"Maybe"—the chameleon's voice was raspy—"we shouldn't think about that too much."

"Why not?"

"Let's take it a day at a time. Can you get enough water from that pipe?"

"Probably. I'm hungry, though."

"You can go a long time without food. Trust me. I lived on bubble gum for a month."

Ruva looked around at the hot, gloomy hold. A few dim lights shone far above. Boxes were stacked on metal racks against the walls. "What if it takes more than a month?"

"I told you, don't think about it! Why are females always so contrary? If I said, 'Don't eat black widow spiders,' you'd whine till you got a bowlful!" Nelson settled deeper into the brackish puddle and closed his eyes.

Ruva explored. At the front of the hold was luggage; in the middle, boxes; at the back were engines, the anchor room, and the elevator. "Where's Troll?"

The chameleon groaned. "How should I know? Probably eating his ratty little heart out in the caviar. He climbed up a pipe to that hatch." The little giraffe looked up to see an opening and the night sky.

"Isn't it better to hunt for food while I'm still strong enough to *disappear*?"

"Another thing about females is that they never shut up. Oh, very well. I'll probably get sprayed with insecticide by those charming Slopes you keep talking about. *You* don't care as long as you stuff yourself." Nelson climbed to Ruva's head and positioned himself between her horns.

Ruva pressed the elevator button with her nose. Her body told her it was the middle of the night, when most humans slept. She moved cautiously through the upper hallway.

The deck was deserted, the sky hung with a thousand winking stars. From several dark doorways, Ruva heard snores. She looked into the dining room window. The tables were littered with the remains of a feast, and Jabila sat, half-dead with weariness, by the kitchen. A heap of bones made the little giraffe shudder.

Ruva almost entered when she became aware that another person was in the room. A six-and-a-half-foot woman, who looked as though she ought to have bolts in her neck, was feeding on cream puffs. She neither spoke nor smiled. She also had a curiously unpleasant way of eating.

The woman inserted her tongue into one end of the cream puff and *sucked*. It sounded like water going down a drainpipe. When the pastry was empty, it was tossed into a heap under the table. The hair stood straight up along Ruva's backbone.

"Stonewall! That's the last cream puff!" Another woman stood in the doorway of the kitchen with her hands on her hips.

Jabila scrambled out of his chair. "There's ice cream in the fridge, Miss Synthia."

"I *hate* ice cream!"

"It's full of lovely chemicals."

"Well . . ."

"It doesn't contain *anything* nutritious," Jabila said temptingly.

Synthia glared at her sister as the boy scurried off. Stonewall sucked the cream out of her pastry with insulting slowness.

Synthia had blond hair and blue eyes. Her long fingernails were painted red. She fluttered them on the table with a sound that reminded Ruva of a porcupine rattling its quills. Synthia was a little *too* perfect: her waist was too tiny for a human, her eyelashes too long, her hair too shiny. In her way, she was more disturbing than Stonewall. She also looked more intelligent.

"You think you can get away with anything because you're Daddy's favorite," Synthia said in a whining, caressing voice.

Stonewall tossed the empty husk under the table.

Jabila came back with two bowls of violently green ice cream. He drenched them with purple syrup that reminded Ruva of the liquid Dante used to keep down fleas. The two demons fed: Stonewall sucked and Synthia took quick, nasty little bites.

Presently, they finished and left. *You don't want to get close to that,* said the giraffe ancestors in

Ruva's mind as the women passed. It was all she could do to keep from bleating.

"So those are Slopes. Females, I see," murmured Nelson.

Jabila slowly began clearing dishes. He dumped the cream-puff husks into a trash can. Troll suddenly poked his nose out from under a chair, and another creature—Ruva's heart turned over—appeared from the kitchen.

"Rodentus!" she cried, stepping through the dining room doorway.

"Ruva, you clever girl. Troll said you were here. Well, well. Let's take a look at you. Do you remember the nine-times table?"

"He made me recite it, too," said Jabila.

"Knowledge is power, young man. Never forget it."

Ruva thought she had never been so happy in her life. Her friend leaped to a table and stood before her. She remembered him, of course, but she had not compared him with another rat before. He was so much more glorious than Troll that they seemed hardly to be the same species.

Hair for hair, whisker for whisker, the two rats were similar, but Troll was a muddy gray while Rodentus gleamed like an autumn wheat field. There hung about him an air of majesty that was hard to describe. He's simply more *there*, Ruva said to herself. She introduced him to Nelson, who merely grunted.

"First things first, my dear," Rodentus said. "I imagine you're hungry."

"Starving," admitted the little giraffe.

Jabila let her clean out the salad bowls. She drank a pitcher of milk and moved on to the cream-puff husks in the trash can.

"Not those," Rodentus said hastily. "You don't want to touch anything Stonewall has been at." Meanwhile, Troll licked out the caviar bowl and nibbled at the bones. Jabila washed the dishes.

Finally, everyone went belowdecks again. Jabila crept into his sleeping bag and was asleep between one breath and the next. The rats went off to explore the ship.

Ruva sighed with happiness. She turned around in the little room, feeling for the Warm Place. When she found it, she stood for a few moments, letting the distant peace of it wash over her. Mother must be thinking about me, she thought.

"It's all right for *you*," grumbled Nelson from a perch on Jabila's sleeping bag. "You got to eat your head off. I haven't had so much as a gnat all day."

Ruva suddenly woke up. She realized she had not seen a single insect since they boarded the *Apocalypso*.

Fourteen

YOU DO UNDERSTAND that you can't run around the ship as though it were a grassland?" said Rodentus. He and the others were crammed into the tiny anchor room. Jabila sat cross-legged on his sleeping bag; Ruva fitted herself between the spool and the wall. Troll watched Rodentus adoringly from her head, and Nelson draped his tail around her neck. The little giraffe didn't know whether he was awake or not. The chameleon had been sunk in gloom all morning.

"I'll bring you food and water here," Jabila said. "I won't be able to do much. The Slopes keep me busy sixteen hours a day, and during breaks I have to study."

"Quite right," said Rodentus. "The important thing to remember is that Slopes go after prey faster than a starving shark gulps a hamburger. But they have weaknesses. They have no imagination, and they don't learn from experience."

"Like all the other poisonous humans," growled Nelson.

"Wrong! To say that is to insult Jabila, who is an excellent person, although ignorant."

"I'm learning," the boy said.

"Of course. I'm an excellent teacher." Rodentus leaped to the top of the spool and sprang from there to a tangle of pipe halfway up the wall. He settled into a comfortable niche, the better to view his audience. "To understand Slopes—and Jabila—you have to go back to the time of King Solomon. Stop fidgeting, Ruva. Your education has holes in it, too. Don't think you can loaf.

"Now," the rat said when everyone was looking at him, "King Solomon was the first human since Babel who could speak the language of the animals. . . ."

THE TALE OF KING SOLOMON AND ASMODEUS
From the Animals' Point of View

Long ago, King Nimrod had been able to speak to animals. That was because he was like an animal. He hunted lions, and they hunted him. He ate when he was hungry, drank when he was thirsty, fell asleep when he was tired—just like the lions.

The World was in balance then, for the most part. But when humans forgot the Common Speech, they began to use the animals as slaves. Understand, I am not saying there was no death. Cats hunted mice, wolves ate lambs, grasshoppers slaughtered grass.

The World is composed of great sorrow and great joy. It has a grandeur beyond anything I can describe, but this I can say: to know what you are and where you belong is the true meaning of Magic.

King Solomon had rings and potions. He called up demons and made them serve him. He thought he understood Magic, but he was only playing with it. For the true and most ancient meaning of Magic is Wisdom.

One day, King Solomon decided to enslave the biggest demon of all, who was named Asmodeus.

Asmodeus lived in a gloomy palace at the roots of the Mountain of Darkness. When he was bored, he kicked the walls to cause earthquakes. When he wished to go forth, he flew in a shower of brimstone from the mouth of a volcano. On returning, the demon quenched his thirst at a great well in his courtyard and slept—uneasily—on a bed of iron.

Solomon sent his servants to the well. They drew out the water and replaced it with wine. Asmodeus returned from a night of blowing dust storms across the Sahara Desert. He drank bucket after bucket of the liquid and fell sound asleep on his iron bed. The servants returned with chains. They bound the demon securely and sealed the locks with Solomon's magic ring. Then they dragged him before the king.

"You sniveling little human!" roared Asmodeus, stamping his clawed feet. "I'll squash you like a grape! I'll drop you into a pool of starving piranhas!"

Solomon tossed the seal ring up and caught it. The demon's bulgy red-veined eyes glittered as they watched. "If I'm not mistaken, you're as helpless as a minnow," the king said. He flicked a few drops of water onto Asmodeus's toes. The water hissed as it turned into steam.

"Interesting," remarked Solomon. And so Asmodeus was harnessed to a boiler. Water was poured over his toes, the steam was channeled into pipes under the floor, and the palace was warmed all winter.

The system worked as long as the demon was angry, and Asmodeus was *always* angry. All he had to do was think of the trick Solomon had played on him. The steam rolled off him in sheets.

One day, Solomon was watching his new heating system in the basement of the palace. Asmodeus, as usual, was chained from neck to ankles with only his claw-tipped toes sticking out. The king tossed the magic seal ring in the air. It turned and caught the light as it fell back into Solomon's hands.

"I have spoken to men and angels," the king said. "I have gained knowledge of the earth, of the lands under the earth, and of high heaven as well."

Toss, glitter, catch. The seal ring went up and down again.

"All things do I know. I am the wisest man who ever lived, and the demons worship and fear me."

Toss, glitter, catch.

"You are not even as bright as Nimrod, and he was dumber than a clam at the bottom of the Red Sea," Asmodeus said in a hissing, creaking voice.

Solomon laughed. *Toss, glitter, catch.*

"Nimrod spoke to lions. He was a king, not a second-rate magician. You ought to put up a tent in the marketplace," snarled Asmodeus.

"I know a thousand times as much as the king of Shinar." Solomon came close to the demon and looked into his red-veined eyes.

"So you say! So you say! The World is covered with lions—and eagles, mice, fish, and fowl. In every part of the earth are creatures you do not understand. You call yourself wise? You know less than the average cattle tick!"

Solomon threw the ring into the air. *Toss, glitter—snap!* Asmodeus's long tongue snaked out and caught it. He tucked it over one fang. The magic seal was broken, and all the demon's strength came back. The chains burst like straw as he began to grow. King Solomon backed away.

"Learn from the animals—by becoming one!" roared Asmodeus. In a trice, Solomon was transformed into a dove. Cooing with fear, the bird dodged around the room until he found a window. Then up he fled into the sky and disappeared among the clouds.

Asmodeus transformed himself into the likeness of the king. He ruled in the place of Solomon. His first act was to take the magic seal ring and throw it into the deepest part of the ocean.

Solomon flew in the shape of a dove until he was exhausted. He fluttered down to a tree. At once, a hawk pounced and carried him off. The king found himself suddenly changed into the hawk. He lived as a fierce hunting bird until he was taken by a fox.

Back and forth went Solomon, from animal to animal. Sometimes he stayed in one body a long time. He took mates and raised young. He hunted and was hunted. Each animal had its own Wisdom to impart. The king was embarrassed when he remembered how he had boasted to the demon.

At last, Solomon found himself in the shape of a whale. He went down to the bottom of the sea, and there he found the seal ring lying in the dark ooze.

He scooped it up in his great mouth, burst to the surface, and swam to shore. He changed himself back to a man and traveled at once to his palace. As he went in the front door, Asmodeus fled out the back in a cloud of smoke and steam.

"My lord, you are so much gentler," cried the courtiers.

"We are no longer afraid of you," cried his wives.

From that time on, Solomon learned not to brag and, especially, not to play catch with his magic ring. He understood the language of animals, and so did his descendants.

Unfortunately, Asmodeus had taken a few wives of his own while he pretended to be king. *His* descendants turned into horrible demons who never learned from experience and who spread misery far and wide throughout the World.

Fifteen

"SLOPES," MURMURED RUVA, resting her head against the iron wall of the anchor room.

"Slopes," agreed Rodentus von Stroheim the Third. "Most humans have both Solomon and Asmodeus as their forebears. A few are pure demons—or Slopes. Jabila is a pure descendant of Solomon."

"That's pretty good." The boy reached up to stroke Nelson's scales absentmindedly.

"You see? Your great-great-great-grandfather wasn't a starving peasant," cried Troll. "What a wonderful story! Oh, it makes me want to go out and do something rash. I think I'll pee in Stonewall's bathwater."

"It's a brave thought, but you must be careful, my friend," Rodentus said. Troll glowed at the praise. He preened his moth-eaten ears and arranged his scabby tail becomingly across his toes.

"Talk, talk, talk," grumbled Nelson. "We're stuck in a miserable hot room surrounded by enemies. I think *that* should be the topic of conversation, not fairy tales about ancient kings."

"You're right." Rodentus stood tall and stern in the tangle of pipes high in the wall. He was closest to the light, and it seemed to Ruva that his fur shone especially brightly.

"Have any of you noticed how humans smell?" the rat asked.

"Horrible!" said Nelson.

"Like dead cats!" cried Troll.

"Wait." Ruva edged from behind the spool. She had to shrink against the wall to avoid stepping on Jabila. "At the zoo, I learned that all humans are different. Some are like hyenas—ugh!—and some like dogs or monkeys. But Jabila's different."

The boy grinned. The little giraffe thought even his flat teeth were somehow attractive.

"Very good, pupil Ruva! Go to the head of the class." Rodentus nodded approvingly. "What you call 'smell' is really *spirit*. Most animals use the wrong word. You are picking up the human soul." He nimbly climbed down the pipes and landed on Jabila's sleeping bag. He looked intently into the boy's eyes before going on.

"It's my belief that humans before the tower of Babel were simply fancy animals. Since then, they've been changing. That's why they smell all wrong.

But now"—the rat hopped to the boy's shoulder and patted his ear fondly—"things are different. Every year more true humans, like Jabila, are born. That isn't surprising. Demons are always getting themselves killed off by their stupid habits. In fact—"

Rodentus leaped to the floor and Troll's fur stood up. Hateful voices approached from the elevator. Both rats began to chitter uncontrollably. Nelson turned lavender, and Ruva stuffed herself into the cramped space behind the spool. Only Jabila kept his head. He went out before Captain Skeekee could come in.

"Move, you gobbet of pond scum!" snarled the captain.

"Let me twist his ears. How I love doing that!" Spongy said. The boy yelped. Footsteps died away, and gradually the animals recovered their calm.

"As I was saying—*chchchch*—drat!—I've been watching the situation for a long time. A week ago, Slippery called all the demons together for an especially big and nasty job. Do you realize that every pure-blooded Slope in the entire World is on board the *Apocalypso* at this moment?" Rodentus paused to let this sink in. The water sloshed and gurgled in the anchor-chain hole.

"Wowie!" murmured Troll at last.

Nelson slowly climbed down Ruva's leg to the sleeping bag. "Are you suggesting we kill them?"

"That would make us no better than they are. We could *trap* them, however," Rodentus said.

"Seems like we're the ones in a trap." The lizard settled himself by Rodentus. Ruva was dismayed to see how thin he had become.

"I have a plan. It's dangerous—"

"We don't care! Let's get the Slopes!" shouted Troll.

"Put grit in their garters
And sand in their socks!
Make holes in their pillows
And fill them with rocks!"

The rat turned a somersault and landed on the sleeping bag. Nelson hissed with irritation as he moved out of the way.

Rodentus smiled. "You don't know what's involved, my friend."

"Count on me! Oh, boy, a dangerous mission!"

"I don't know which is worse: sneaky rats or stupid ones," the chameleon said.

"Sh!" Rodentus held up a paw. Heavy footsteps approached from outside. The rats melted into the shadows; Nelson faded into the sleeping bag. The door opened, and Stonewall peered in. She licked her lips with a long, thin tongue that had a barb at the tip.

The little giraffe trembled as she gazed at the demon. All of her head and several inches of neck were clearly visible over the spool. Stonewall gazed into the room for a long moment. Then she lumbered off. Ruva began to whimper with fright.

"It's all right. She didn't see you," whispered Rodentus.

"I don't see why not," Nelson said. "The stupid giraffe practically jumped up and down for attention. Females always fall apart when the going gets rough."

"I don't get it," said Troll.

"That's the wonderful thing about Slopes," Rodentus explained. "They have absolutely no imagination. The last thing Stonewall expected to see was a giraffe, and so she *couldn't* see one."

"I think it's dumb to walk around at all in a boat full of demons. Wake me when it gets dark." The chameleon waddled to an oily puddle and lowered himself with a sigh. "Slopes everywhere... crazy rats... hysterical females..." Grumbling softly, the lizard closed his eyes and fell asleep.

R UVA'S MOUTH was as dry as cotton by late afternoon. Finally, she couldn't bear it any longer and ventured out to find the leaky pipe. The water dripped with agonizing slowness. She licked it morosely as she thought of the pitchers in the dining room. The little giraffe stood in deep shadow behind a metal rack of boxes.

The elevator door suddenly opened and two Slopes came out. Ruva recognized Sargon from Rodentus's description. He was as squat as a tank, and his curved toenails were distinctly green. He shifted boxes under the direction of Synthia.

She gave orders in a voice that made Ruva's nerves flutter. It was *too* sweet, like a long, slow drip of honey. Ruva could almost see it oozing around her feet.

She stood as still as possible as the Slopes passed within inches of her. *Help!* cried the giraffe ancestors, fleeing across distant grasslands in her mind. The odor of nameless dead things from the roots of mountains curled around her nose. She was shivering uncontrollably by the time the demons left.

Sixteen

"HOW CAN YOU stand them?" Ruva asked Jabila. Rodentus had called them together one morning to discuss his plan.

The boy shrugged. "I got used to them. The first week I couldn't keep anything in my stomach."

"I'd like the chance to keep something in my stomach," Nelson moaned. His skin was dull gray instead of the dark green of the sleeping bag, where he was resting. He no longer had the energy to change color.

"Can't you help him?" Ruva asked.

"Everything's soaked with insecticide," said Jabila.

"I dream of mole crickets," whispered the chameleon. "Lovely, fat African mole crickets. I can hear them chirping even now."

They were silent for a few moments after that. Rodentus led them to the center of the hold. A single heavily wrapped box sat on a rack high above the damp floor. The rat climbed up and found a pencil, which he used as a pointer.

"Have you ever heard of the Sargasso Strangleweed?" he said, tapping the box.

"No, but you're going to tell us, whether we want to know or not," said Nelson.

"Quite right. The Sargasso Strangleweed, scientific name *Strangula omniverans*, is the most aggressive plant in the World. Drop one in a forest, and it will pull down every tree in an hour. It can suck a lake dry faster than it takes Stonewall to empty a bag of cream puffs. *Strangula* is too tough to eat, too rubbery to build with, and too wet for firewood."

"Sounds like something the Slopes would love," remarked Jabila.

"You said it. Slippery and his clan have been collecting Strangleweed seeds for a long time. *There's enough in that box to blight an entire continent!*"

"Wowie!" Troll cried.

"Slippery plans to drop them on Africa. He has hundreds of warehouses full of stale cornmeal. Once all the crops are destroyed, he'll sell the cornmeal to African governments in exchange for diamonds."

"Excuse me," said Ruva. "If this plant is so bad, why hasn't it taken over before?"

"Excellent question, pupil Ruva." Rodentus tucked the pencil under his arm. "The World is in balance, my dear. As long as the Strangleweeds stay in their natural home—which is the Sargasso Sea—they are fed upon by Gross Green Sea-Going Sargasso Snails. Strangleweeds grow at lightning speed, but Gross Green Sea-Going Sargasso Snails eat them faster than nuclear-powered vacuum cleaners."

"That's lucky," said Jabila.

"Fortunately, we will pass through the Sargasso Sea in a few hours. It's the only safe place to dump the seeds."

"A wonderful plan!" shouted Troll. He bounded up a metal rack and banged it like a drum.

"Shut up, you maniac!" Nelson hissed. Jabila grabbed the rat and smoothed his fur. Troll continued beating time on the boy's fist.

"There's more," Rodentus said. "It's no good merely dumping the seeds. Slippery will only harvest more. We have to pour water on the box here. The weeds will grow over the ship and anchor it to the middle of the Sargasso Sea—forever!"

"I love it!" shrieked Troll. Jabila tried to cover his mouth, but the rat nipped him.

"If—they're trapped, so are we," faltered Ruva.

"They'll have to eat Gross Green Sea-Going Sargasso Snails!" Troll was overcome with giggles.

Nelson groaned. "If the Slopes get hungry, the first thing they're going to eat is giraffe steaks, followed by ratburgers."

"I'll never see Mother again," Ruva wailed.

"Pay attention!" Rodentus said sternly. "It's all a matter of planning. I'll bite through the radio wires so they can't call for help. Troll will chew open the box, and Ruva will dump water on it. Jabila will launch the lifeboat. We can escape if we time it exactly right."

"And if we don't?" Nelson swiveled both eyes to focus on the rat.

Rodentus stood straight and tall. His vibrissae radiated like the rays of a sun in a painting. "Wouldn't it be a noble thing to rid the World of Slopes forever?"

"Not at the risk of being made into chameleon tacos by demons! Of all the loony schemes—nobody but baby giraffes and half-baked humans would believe—typical rat nonsense—" Nelson stopped to catch his breath. His sides heaved.

Troll wriggled out of Jabila's grasp and slithered to the floor. "They'll talk about us wherever animals gather," he cried, dancing around the lizard. "They'll call us the Five Heroes—is that right?" He paused to count on his toes. "One, two—um, yes, *Five* Heroes. Think of it, Nelson! Lady Gila monsters will line up to groom your scales."

"Count me out! I'm going to find a hole to waste away in, in peace." Nelson's voice became wistful. "I'm going to dream of beautiful fat African mole crickets." He found a gap between two metal plates in the side of the ship, eased himself inside, and refused to talk anymore.

"He's irritable because he's so hungry," whispered Ruva.

"We'll come and get you when the lifeboat's ready," Troll said. Nelson only wedged himself in deeper and closed his eyes.

Rodentus made them memorize the steps of the plan. "We'll have only a few minutes to get away. Once the weeds cover the ship, we'll be trapped. Troll has to chew open the box *after* we reach the Sargasso Sea. If he does it too soon, the rolling of the ship may spill out a seed and alert the Slopes."

"How will we know when it's time?" asked the little giraffe.

"Do you feel how the ship rolls from side to side?" Jabila said.

Ruva did now that she thought about it. The movement was so steady she hadn't noticed it.

"In the Sargasso the water is still. If you leaned over the side, your face would be perfectly reflected."

"How interesting!"

"All you'll feel is the vibration of the engines." Jabila stroked Ruva's fur as he spoke. If it had been any other human she would have been frightened.

"When we're ready on deck, Jabila will blow a whistle down the hatch. You two—" Rodentus tapped his pencil against a shelf. Troll stopped picking his teeth and snapped to attention. "You two," Rodentus continued, "will perform your tasks as though your lives depended on them. And they do."

Jabila showed them a rusted faucet near the engine room. "This drains seawater from the boilers." He banged it with a wrench. Flecks of metal showered on the floor.

"Don't hit it too hard," warned Rodentus. Ruva was able to work it open. She practiced carrying a bucket with her mouth. This was a lot harder than she expected. She made many mistakes and splashed water everywhere.

"Remember to turn the faucet off afterward. You don't want the seeds to grow too fast," muttered Rodentus. "I estimate you have five minutes to get to the elevator before it's blocked off. Perhaps you should make that *four* minutes."

Ruva felt queasy.

She practiced until her jaws ached. Troll chewed holes in other boxes to get into shape. Finally, Rodentus was satisfied.

"Remember," he warned them as he left, "there's no safety margin. If you're too late, well . . ."

"You can count on us," said Troll.

"I'll bring Nelson," Ruva told him.

Rodentus looked at her a long moment before he spoke. "He might refuse to come."

"I couldn't leave him!"

"I'll pull him out by the tail," promised Troll.

"I wish I had time to explain about chameleons," Rodentus said. "They have extremely strong wills. If Nelson wants to stay, I'm not sure you *can* move him."

"Leave it to me, boss. I'll tell him the Gila monster wants to move in."

Rodentus smiled at his friend. "Just don't do anything foolish."

"Wouldn't dream of it. Rat's honor." Troll held up his left paw with the fingers crossed.

Seventeen

RUVA WAITED in the anchor room. For the first time the heat and motion of the boat made her seasick, and she had to admit she was frightened as well. What if they didn't get away? What if they were trapped with the hungry demons? The memory of the bones she had seen in the dining room came back to haunt her. She fell into an uneasy sleep. In her dreams she was pursued by the visitors to the zoo, but they had turned into a pack of animals.

They weren't true animals. The monkeys had claws and the antelopes had fangs. The lions, on the other hand, ran on soft, fleshy feet. They gnashed horrible flat teeth at her.

"Come back! Come back!" cried the misshapen creatures. "We have forgotten what it is to be wild, and our cities frighten us. Please teach us what it is to be animals again!"

They burst into howls, barks, snarls, and screams. Ruva skidded along a cement walk. She leaped a low hedge and splashed into the flamingo pond. A high piercing whistle rose above the other sounds. She threw her head to one side—

—and banged it against the metal wall of the anchor room. The whistle stopped abruptly. It was Jabila! The ship was moving steadily ahead. They were in the Sargasso Sea, and she was supposed to pour water on the seeds right now!

Ruva galloped out of the anchor room, found the faucet, and turned it on. She heard Captain Skeekee shout, "You little pimple! What were you doing with that whistle?" Jabila cried out as he was struck. The hatch above was open, and she could see Spongy and Stonewall standing by it.

"That wasn't in the plan," Ruva gasped. When the bucket was full, she tried to turn off the faucet. The rusted metal cracked, and water spurted across the floor. "It's all going wrong," she whimpered.

"Hurry!" shrieked Troll. He was wedged behind Nelson in the hole. The chameleon had puffed himself up. "Tickle, tickle," warbled the rat, digging his paws into Nelson's scales. "You may be able to stand pain, but *nobody* can put up with tickling." The chameleon hissed, and his eyes bugged out.

Ruva saw the box on the high shelf. Troll had cut the top neatly away. Inside nestled gray-green seeds the size of pearls. She had only to tip the bucket over them.

"Hhhaaaahhrrr," came a chorus of snarls from above. In spite of herself, Ruva jerked up her head. Water sloshed over her neck. Looking down the hatch were Synthia, Sargon, Spongy, Captain Skeekee, and Stonewall. Behind them was something—just a glimpse of something—that froze Ruva's blood. The water shook in the bucket.

"Hurry!" yelled Troll.

Ruva forced herself to move. At that instant Stonewall swung through the hatch. She moved from pipe to pipe as easily as a gibbon in a tree and landed with a *whump* right in front of the little giraffe. Ruva dropped the bucket. She couldn't help it. Stonewall's flat eyes paralyzed her as surely as if she had come face-to-face with a moray eel.

"Protect the seeds!" shouted Synthia from above. Stonewall licked her lips. Ruva stood perfectly still, willing herself to *disappear*, but she couldn't do it: her mind was frozen with terror. She felt water swirling around her feet from the broken faucet.

"Forget the giraffe!" Synthia screamed.

"Gotcha!" Troll yelled as Nelson scrambled out of his hiding place. The two jumped into the water. The rat reached the shelf and scurried up as fast as he could go. The chameleon wriggled until he reached Ruva's ankle, where he clamped himself on like a leech.

"Stonewall, you goat-head! *Now* isn't the time

to feed!" Synthia screeched as the demon reached for Ruva. The barbed tongue twitched out of her mouth. Troll streaked across the top of the shelf, threw himself at the box, and tipped it over. Gray-green pearls showered onto the floor.

"Nooooo!" moaned the demons gathered at the hatch.

Troll's momentum carried him too far. He tried to hold on, but the seeds rolled under his paws. He fell with a startled squeak. Down he went and bounced off Stonewall's broad shoulder. The demon instinctively flicked her tongue at him. Then he tumbled the rest of the way to the floor.

Or what had been the floor.

It was now a rolling mass of gray-green tendrils. Higher and higher they rose as the Sargasso Strangleweeds drank the water that poured from the faucet. As the tendrils grew, they became thicker. From the size of hairs, they swelled until they were as thick as fire hoses. Leathery gray-green leaves sprouted from the sides. One of them slapped Ruva in the face.

Ruva snatched up Troll in her mouth. She floundered like a swimmer and somehow, with great effort, managed to stay on top of the growing plants. Nelson clung to her ankle and cursed every time she moved her feet.

Stonewall was unable to see the wisdom of Ruva's behavior. She could have climbed back to the hatch with ease, but that was not her way. She threw herself at the vines, kicking and biting viciously; they roped around her body as they grew. In a very few minutes they had covered her so completely, Ruva could only see a heaving leafy mass. Now and then a clump of vines bulged out, as though the demon were still battling away inside.

As Rodentus had said, Stonewall had no imagination.

The little giraffe saw she was in danger of being crushed against the ceiling. With a last burst of energy, she wriggled along until she was just able to squeeze under the hatch. Then she didn't have to move at all. The Strangleweeds carried her out.

She felt herself picked up and flung over someone's shoulder. She had a quick impression of Spongy and Captain Skeekee hacking at the vines with axes. The instant they severed one, another grew in its place. "Get to the fallout shelter!" cried Synthia.

Ruva was bounced along with Troll still in her mouth. She hoped she wasn't holding him too tightly. She recognized Sargon's scaly green heels as the demon pounded along. Presently she was dumped onto the floor of a gray room.

Poor Troll dropped out of her mouth and lay motionless. Ruva's tongue felt funny. Her head was spinning. She heard the Slopes grumbling as they moved around.

"Seal the door!" commanded Synthia. "I'll turn on the emergency air tanks."

"Stonewall's out there," Captain Skeekee objected.

"That's her problem."

"You always hated Stonewall because she's better-looking," said Spongy in a nasty whining voice.

"She can eat two cows at a sitting. You can only manage one," Sargon said.

"Seal the door!" came a new voice Ruva had never heard. It was so filled with malice and cruelty, the other demons turned pale green. Sargon quickly slammed the door. He turned a wheel to lock it. Synthia pushed a button, and air began to blow through a vent.

"I get Stonewall's rations," announced Spongy. A long tentacle reached out and slapped him. The demon squealed, "Don't hit me! I'll be good!"

"Baaaaad, you mean," said the terrifying new voice.

"Yes, Daddy," sniveled Spongy.

Then everything was quiet except for the far-away booming of the Strangleweeds as they pinned the *Apocalypso* to the middle of the Sargasso Sea.

Eighteen

GRADUALLY RUVA'S WITS returned. Her mouth was still numb, but her head had stopped swimming. They were in a medium-sized room with no windows. In a corner were stacked many boxes. A dim light shone in the center of the ceiling.

Not far away sat Sargon, Synthia, Spongy, and Captain Skeekee. Beside them was someone else Ruva refused to look at. She caught only a glimpse of a monstrous ear crusted with oozing scales. It looked slimy and greasy at the same time.

Ruva moved her head cautiously. There, to her dismay, was Jabila. He was tied up and had a gag in his mouth. Next to him was a large cast-iron pot. Out of the corner of her eye she saw Troll lying on his back with a bloody streak across his chest. His tail twitched feebly. *Stonewall's barbed tongue must have poisoned him,* the little giraffe thought in horror.

"How long can we stay in here?" Sargon's harsh voice boomed.

"Two weeks," Synthia replied. "Then everything runs out."

"Can we radio for help?"

"We could have until a certain rat—*hisssss*—chewed through the wires." Synthia lifted the lid of the cast-iron pot. Rodentus stood up and coolly regarded the demons.

That's the end of it, thought Ruva. They've got *him.* There's no hope.

Rodentus suddenly noticed Troll. He jumped out of the pot and ran to him. Captain Skeekee raised his arm to throw a knife, but Synthia stopped him. "Food keeps better if it's alive," she said.

Rodentus bustled around, feeling Troll's head and taking his pulse. "Bad luck, eh?" he said.

"Bad luck," agreed Troll. His voice was so faint, Ruva felt like crying.

Rodentus sniffed the bloody scratch. "What happened here?" He might have been sharing a rice cracker with the Dalai Lama instead of being trapped in a fallout shelter with demons.

"Stonewall . . . ," Troll whispered. He was unable to go on. Ruva sat up under the watchful gaze of several pairs of red-veined eyes. Nelson unclamped his feet and dropped to the floor. Her leg was sore where he had hung on.

"He fell onto Stonewall's shoulder," the little giraffe said. Rodentus listened attentively as she explained. When she described how Troll had knocked over the seeds, all the Slopes drew in their breath. They sounded like boilers overloading with steam.

"So Stonewall poisoned him," Rodentus said.

"I'm afraid so."

Rodentus was about to say more when Spongy suddenly announced, "I'm hungry!"

"You're always hungry," growled Captain Skeekee.

"I'm really, really, really hungry *now*."

"We have to ration food," Synthia said.

"Since when does a demon ration anything?"

Rodentus found an old sock on the floor and dragged it over to cover Troll. The injured rat was shivering although the air in the fallout shelter was uncomfortably warm.

"You know, Spongy's right," Sargon remarked. "Only stupid humans plan for the future. Slopes always enjoy themselves as soon as possible. If we have to wait even a minute to have fun, we throw tantrums."

"That's right," agreed Captain Skeekee.

"There are five of us and five of them." Spongy stood up, and his flesh quivered around inside his uniform. "I'm the hungriest so I get to eat the biggest one."

"I'm the smartest so *I* get first pick," Synthia said.

"I'm the ugliest!" cried Sargon.

"I'm the nastiest!" yelled Captain Skeekee.

"And I'm the baaaaadest!"

Everyone stopped at once. The fifth Slope, old Slippery himself, uncurled from where he had been sitting. He towered above the others.

"I kick baby robins out of nests and feed sour milk to kittens. I'm the baaaaadest demon that ever was—and I'm going to eat the giraffe for lunch right now!"

Ruva began to whimper with terror. Slippery was covered with tentacles instead of arms. He had two trunklike legs from which the toes splayed like the arms of starfish. His head was shaped like a turnip, and his skin gave off a stench of sulfur.

"You're also the stuuuuupidest demon who ever lived," Rodentus said calmly.

Sargon, Synthia, Spongy, Captain Skeekee, and Slippery turned to look at him. The rat stood up on his hind legs. His fur gleamed with a light that reminded Ruva of tall golden grass.

"How long do you think the food in this shelter will last?" Rodentus said. "Two weeks? Hah! With your habits, two days. And what then? Who will be on the menu next? Spongy?" The fat demon moved away from the others. "Or will it be Synthia or Sargon?"

All the Slopes began to eye one another uneasily. Captain Skeekee took out his knife and cleaned his claws thoughtfully.

"I can tell you right now who will be last,"

continued Rodentus. "Dear old Slippery. Well, that's not my concern. I've done what I set out to do, which was to rid the World of Slopes."

"*I'll still be left. You said so,*" Slippery objected.

"Oh, yes. The stuuuuupidest demon in the World will be sitting on top of a heap of weeds in the middle of the Sargasso Sea, getting hungrier . . . and hungrier . . . and hungrier."

"*Then I'd better eat right now before it's too late! I'll start with the giraffe and have the boy next. The rats and the chameleon can be dessert—*"

"Nobody is eating chameleons for dessert or anything else!" shouted Nelson. Ruva, who had been hypnotized by the conversation, suddenly noticed that Nelson had walked to the middle of the floor. He stood between them and the Slopes. He was terribly thin, but rage had puffed him up. His skin was purple, and his eyes bugged out like grapes. He looked not unlike a small demon himself.

"You! Slopes! Back against the wall! Don't make me any angrier or I'll put a spell on you!"

The demons snickered, a horrid sizzling sound.

"Don't make me lose my temper!"

"Ooo, I'm shaking all over," said Spongy.

"Please, Mr. Chameleon. Don't bite us," Sargon said. The other Slopes howled with laughter.

"*Wait!*" Slippery snapped his tentacles for attention. "*The lizard's too small for the main course and too tough for dessert. Let's make him into a taco!*"

How the Slopes howled then! They slapped their knees and stamped their feet. Synthia produced some extremely unladylike snorts. They didn't pay attention to Nelson, but Ruva did. She had seen him turn purple, but never this color. It was darker, and yet hotter and more dangerous. She held her breath. Darker and hotter grew the chameleon. The air vibrated around him.

"That's—*it!*" Nelson hissed. "*Nobody's* going to make a taco out of *me!*"

Nelson advanced on the demons, and presently their laughter died down to giggles. The giggles turned into hiccups and faded away completely. Red-veined eyes watched the lizard approach. Sargon licked his lips.

Ruva thought she would scream. Any second now, one of the Slopes would pounce. Nelson was almost within reach of Slippery's tentacles. Then, suddenly—it was hard to tell exactly when—the demons began to look different. They weren't as frightening as before. They were . . . smaller.

Ruva could hardly believe it. The Slopes were shrinking! And at the same time they were *changing*. Synthia turned squat and fat; Spongy's head—never attractive—became little and hard. Captain Skeekee's color deepened to a greenish brown. Sargon's arms flattened, and Slippery's tentacles simply shrank up into his body and disappeared.

All the while they were growing smaller. Soon they were the size of turkeys, then chickens. They became as small as mice, and finally, when they were no bigger than bumblebees, they stopped shrinking.

They looked like mole crickets.

Fat African mole crickets.

"Close your eyes, Ruva. You don't want to see this," murmured Rodentus.

She obeyed. She tried not to listen, but a certain *gallump*—repeated five times—sent shivers down her spine. After a while she opened her eyes again.

All of the mole crickets were gone.

Nelson sat in the middle of the floor. His color was a normal gray-brown. His sides bulged, and his eyes were closed. "I feel *wonderful*," he sighed.

"That was the stuuuuupidest demon in the World," said Rodentus. "Never, never try to make tacos out of chameleons. Now, Ruva, my dear, see if you can find a medical kit. I'll chew through Jabila's ropes. We'll need him to use it."

Nineteen

CRITCHY-SCRATCHY noises came from beyond the sealed door as the Strangleweeds rustled past. The ship quivered delicately. Ruva looked through the supplies until she found a small case labeled "First Aid." She brought it over to Troll. By that time, Jabila's hands were free. He was able to remove the rest of the ropes and the gag from his mouth.

"At last!" he cried. "Ptoo! That was Sargon's pocket handkerchief." He opened the medical kit and found disinfectant. He gently cleaned Troll's chest. "I've seen Stonewall inject her prey with poison before she eats it. I can kill the germs, but I'm afraid . . . well, I'm just afraid." The rat moaned and opened his eyes.

"O Tawny Prince," he said in a faint voice.

"Yes, my friend," said Rodentus.

"I have fought the good fight. I have battled the enemy and won."

"I know," Rodentus said gently.

"You should have seen the Slopes when I knocked over the box of seeds." Troll looked a little more alert. "Oh my, they practically wet their pants."

"It was well done," said Rodentus.

"Was it a great prank?"

"Great, indeed!"

Troll coughed and his whole body shuddered. "I would have liked to follow you on your adventures, but . . ." He was too weak to go on.

"I understand."

Ruva began to whimper. Jabila's eyes filled with tears, and even Nelson looked upset. "Oh, please, Troll! Try to live! I'll miss you so much!" cried Ruva.

"Don't leave us," begged Jabila.

"Stick around," Nelson said.

"I'm sorry," whispered Troll. " 'The Five Heroes' had such a ring to it. Now it—it will have to be the *Four* Heroes. Farewell, comrades. I was lucky . . . to have . . . such devoted friends." His eyes closed. He shivered once and was still.

"I never thought the poison was so strong," said Rodentus in a quiet voice.

"You mean—he *can't* be," gasped Ruva.

"He was the bravest of us all," Jabila said with the tears rolling down his face.

[114]

"Boagh! Boagh! He was such a wonderful friend," Ruva bleated. "Oh, it's so unfair!"

"I should have been nicer to him," moaned Nelson, curling himself into a ball. "When he tickled me, I called him a—well, never mind what I called him. He was only trying to help. Poor, brave, handsome Troll! I'll miss him forever!"

Troll opened one eye. "You think I'm handsome?"

There was a shocked silence.

Ruva gulped and saw that Troll was shivering all over, but not from shock or cold. He was trying to keep from laughing out loud.

"You lousy, stinking, miserable, lying rat!" screamed Nelson.

"Oh, Nelson, you really care!" Troll lost the battle and began shrieking with laughter. "Oh my! That was good! 'I'll miss you forever.' "

"I'll miss you because I'm going to kill you all over again!"

"Gently, gently," said Rodentus, coming between the enraged lizard and Troll.

"No chameleon would play such a stupid trick!" Nelson shouted.

"Troll would make a very bad chameleon—," Rodentus began. Then he grinned in a way that cheered Ruva in spite of all the recent danger and fear. "But he makes an *excellent* rat." He and Troll fell into each other's arms with squeals of joy.

"Did you hear? He asked me to stick around," gasped Troll.

"And you did! You did!" howled Rodentus. They chittered and danced, pounded each other on the back, and finally wound up on the floor, wheezing with mirth.

"I hate rats!" Nelson stalked off to a corner and turned his back. "Crazy overgrown mice," he muttered. "Ought to stay in the dump. Never take life seriously."

Jabila and Ruva were too happy to be annoyed. "You certainly fooled me," the boy said. "I've often seen Stonewall sting her prey. How did you survive?"

"I couldn't move at first, but it wore off," Troll replied.

"My mouth was numb! I must have touched the poison when I picked you up." Ruva lowered her head so the rat could climb aboard. He draped himself between her horns.

"Stonewall injects her prey with a narcotic to keep it still," Rodentus explained. "She prefers live food."

"That means—as soon as I was paralyzed—she would have eaten me. Ick!" cried Troll.

"Next time I'll loan her salt and pepper," Nelson growled from his corner.

JABILA opened the boxes with Captain Skeekee's pocketknife. Besides bottles of water, he unpacked chocolate bars, canned fruit, and milk. Ruva would be able to survive on these. Jabila unwrapped

Meals-Ready-to-Eat from army rations for himself, Rodentus, and Troll. They didn't find any insects, but Nelson said he wouldn't be hungry for a while.

"Do ships usually have fallout shelters?" Ruva asked. She inserted her tongue into one of the cans of peaches that Jabila had opened with a can opener attached to Captain Skeekee's knife. The top was surrounded with jagged metal. It was something like pulling acacia leaves out from between thorns.

"The Slopes liked to watch nuclear tests in the South Seas. It was their idea of a vacation," said Jabila. "They used to cheer when the mushroom cloud went up, but of course not even demons like radiation. They waited in here until things cooled down. This room is bulletproof, bombproof, and—fortunately for us—weedproof." Everyone stopped to listen. The slithering, booming sound of the vines could be heard over the whisper from the air vent.

"Strangleweed roots feed on most vegetable matter if they have enough water," said Rodentus. He climbed to the top of a box and tapped his foot for attention.

"Not lessons *now*," said Jabila.

"I have no patience with ignorance. Or did you have something more important to do than stuff yourself with Meals-Ready-to-Eat?"

"No," sighed Jabila.

"Good. Given enough water, Strangleweeds will attack compost, paper, cardboard, and even cotton sheets."

"How about wood?" Ruva asked.

[117]

"Good point, pupil Ruva. They have to be very hungry to eat wood, but they'll do it eventually."

"How much of this ship is wood?"

"A lot," Jabila said gloomily.

"If it wasn't for certain pea-brained rats, we'd be on our way to Africa right now," said Nelson. "But no. *They* had to save the World. They had to do something heroic and drag *me* along with them."

All around, the vines slithered like thousands of snakes restlessly hunting for mice. Sometimes they leaned against the door and tried to push it open.

"Won't they ever stop? It's like being buried alive!" Jabila said in a voice dangerously close to panic.

"Eventually they'll run out of water," Rodentus said. "Then, if they behave like most plants, they'll send their roots looking for more. That means the sea. Frankly, I don't know what to expect then. It's possible, with the vines hanging all over the ship, that they will simply pull us under the water."

"Isn't that just a typical example of rat planning?" groaned Nelson.

Ruva listened anxiously to the boom and slither of the Strangleweeds. Now and then the ship trembled. Her heart raced with fear.

"What kind of spell did you cast on the Slopes, Nelson?" Jabila asked. "I didn't know Magic really existed."

"Really existed!" Rodentus cried indignantly. "Where were you brought up? Why the World is steeped in Magic. A seed of it lies at the heart of every living thing. You can't see it because you don't believe it's there, any more than Stonewall could see Ruva."

"I'm sorry," said Jabila.

"No, no. I shouldn't be impatient. Of course you should ask questions if you don't know something. Let me explain about Nelson—"

"Nobody needs to explain anything about me," said the chameleon.

"Oh, but I do, for you are a most wonderful creation with abilities beyond the common run of animals, even though you are too thickheaded to appreciate it." Rodentus bowed gracefully. Nelson, unable to sort out the compliment from the insult, snapped his mouth shut and bugged out his eyes in frustration.

"Chameleons are the masters of change," the rat explained. "They *disappear* better than any living thing. The reason for this goes back almost to the beginning of time. . . ."

Twenty

LONG AGO, when there were giants in the World and the forests were inhabited by unicorns, there lived a man called Noah," Rodentus began.

"He built the ark," Jabila said.

"Yes, indeed. That was before the days of King Nimrod. Humans and animals still understood the Common Speech. The humans had been getting wickeder and wickeder—"

"They were never good for much," remarked Nelson.

"The chameleons weren't any better. Keep quiet."

Nelson stumped off to an overturned box and crawled inside. Ruva noticed that he turned sideways to listen.

THE STORY OF NOAH'S ARK
From the Animals' Point of View

In those faraway days at the beginning of the World, the humans had all become wicked except for Noah and his family. The animals were wicked, too. Everyone had forgotten what he or she was and where he or she belonged. Everything was out of balance. Violence was everywhere: there were bad elephants, bad dogs, even bad gnats.

In the midst of all this Noah began to build the ark. He sent messages by the birds for the animals to gather. A Flood was coming, he said. It was a Flood such as no one had ever seen or even dreamed of. The animals had better hurry because he had room for only two of each kind on his ship.

"What if thousands come? How will I choose?" he asked Mrs. Noah.

"Wait and see. Things have a way of working out more smoothly than you expect," she replied.

She was correct. When the birds sang in the hills, valleys, and fields, most of the animals ignored them. "Go away!" trumpeted the bad elephants. "We're squashing watermelons so no one can eat them."

"Push off!" growled the bad dogs. "We're taking children for walks to lose them in the woods."

"Scram!" whined the bad gnats. "We're waiting in a swarm to beat up butterflies."

Only two of each kind of animal listened—exactly the right number to fill the ark—except for the chameleons. A thousand of them answered the call. Two were kind and gentle. The other nine hundred and ninety-eight were wicked.

"Selfish humans," the bad ones said. "They're going to have a wild party on that boat, and we intend to crash it."

"How will you get on?" asked the two good chameleons, whose names were Scale and Petal.

"We'll *disappear*. Noah's six hundred years old. His eyesight's so bad, he won't catch us."

The ark took several months to finish and several more for Noah and his sons to fill with grain, fruit, and vegetables, and with mealworms for the insect eaters. The lizards practiced turning different colors. They trained themselves to look like tiger stripes, elephant hide, and leopard spots.

When the day came, the sky filled with ominous black clouds. Thunder growled in every direction. Noah and his sons began to ferry animals into the ark.

First came the elephants. Noah greeted them, and they waved their trunks solemnly. He didn't notice that a small elephant-colored

lizard clung to each gray leg. Eight of the bad
chameleons got on board that way. Then eight
hippopotamus-colored chameleons, eight
rhinoceros-colored ones, and eight buffalo-
colored ones sneaked in.

The weather, meanwhile, was getting
worse. Rain fell in great black sheets in the
distance. Lightning jittered from hill to hill.

"Hurry up!" shouted Noah. "The storm's
almost here!" The wind howled. It bent the
trees with a terrifying crackling sound. The
remaining animals ran for their lives.

Scale and Petal waddled as fast as they
could. Their feet didn't work well on flat
ground. They patiently made their way among
the scurrying feet of goats, deer, rabbits, and
turkeys. Big drops of water pelted them. "Do
you think we should tell Noah about the
others?" whispered Scale.

"It's too late now," Petal whispered back.

The rain poured down like swimming
pools being emptied from heaven. Noah
scooped up Scale and Petal and raced for the
door. His sons slammed it and sealed it with
pitch. The ark rose onto the Flood with its
timbers groaning. The wind buffeted it from
side to side. The animals howled with fear.
Even the humans clung to one another and
yelled every time a big wave threatened to
knock them over.

Finally, after a long, long time, Noah and

his family went around to be sure no one was hurt. "Where are the unicorns?" asked Mrs. Noah.

Everyone searched the ark from top to bottom. All the stalls were occupied; all the storerooms were full. In the space that should have belonged to the unicorns were the nine hundred and ninety-eight bad chameleons. "This is terrible! Everything's out of balance," Noah cried.

"Wait and see. Things have a way of working out more smoothly than you expect," said Mrs. Noah.

So there they all were, tossed hither and yon on the deepest ocean the World has ever seen. "This is a lousy party," complained the chameleons. "Where's the entertainment? Where's the booze? We're bored." It was cold and wet. Most of the animals were seasick. For forty days and forty nights the storm raged on, and then it stopped. The humans and animals looked out on a World from which every scrap of land had disappeared.

Now came the time of waiting as the ocean dried up. Each day the land came closer to the surface, but the animals didn't know that. All they could see was water. Their legs ached with the desire to run. Their dreams were full of green fields. The bad chameleons carried gossip from one end of the ship to the other.

"Did you know," they whispered to the buffalo, "that the elephants get *twice* as much food as you?" "Do you realize," they whispered to the elephants, "that the buffalo have *fresh* grass instead of hay? That's because Noah likes them better." Up and down and round about they went, until the whole ark hummed with irritation.

The lions were the easiest to fool. All a chameleon had to say was "Noah's bringing you an antelope for dinner!" and the lions would run back and forth with their tongues hanging out. The lizards used the same trick over and over. The big cats never caught on.

"I want an antelope!" roared the lion one day.

"They brought us oatmeal again," said the lioness, sniffing at the food bowl.

"I don't expect a *whole* antelope," the lion said reasonably. "A leg would do."

"Get away!" said the antelopes, lowering their horns.

"We promised not to hunt. We promised to be good." The lynx and panthers lapped at their porridge.

"I wonder," said the lion. "Couldn't we be bad a few minutes and make up for it later?"

"Get away!" said the cows, horses, and sheep, stamping their hooves.

"You know why we can't hunt," a tigress growled. "There are only two of each kind aboard. If we ate anyone, we'd destroy a whole species."

The lion thought very hard. It was a new thing for him and it hurt. His forehead rumpled. Jagged streaks of light appeared before his eyes. "There are two of us and the antelope and—ow!—the sheep and so on. *But there are lots and lots of chameleons.*"

The panthers, tigers, lynx, bears, wolves, and jaguars looked at one another thoughtfully.

From then on it was open season on the chameleons. They could *disappear* for a while, but sooner or later they had to sleep. The minute one of them nodded off, he appeared. And so did a panther, tiger, lynx, bear, wolf, jaguar, or lion. Soon there were only two chameleons left: Scale and Petal.

"I can't stay awake another minute," Scale moaned.

"Try, darling," whispered Petal. "We have to find land soon." But poor Scale was exhausted. He closed his eyes, and presently his skin, which had blended with the brown wall, turned gray with sleep.

"Gotcha!" yelled the lion, pinning Scale to the deck with his paw.

"Stop!" screamed Petal. "We're the only chameleons left!"

"There's tons of chameleons. I've been eating them for days."

"That's why there aren't any more!" Petal cried desperately.

"She's right," said the tigress. "If you eat him, you'll destroy the whole species."

"Nuts to that. I'll apologize later."

"If you don't stop, I'll put a spell on you!" screamed Petal. She turned purple with rage. Her eyes bugged out like grapes. The tigress sat down on her tail, she was so surprised. The lion hesitated with his paw on Scale.

Petal turned a deeper purple. She seemed to get hotter. The air around her vibrated. All the animals watched in amazement as the little chameleon changed. Then, when it seemed she couldn't get any darker, the *lion* began to change. He began to shrink. Scale wriggled out of his grasp and scuttled to safety.

And still the air hummed with energy, and Petal glowed like a hot black coal. The lion shrank until he was the size of a cub. Then Petal began to cool down. She went from deep purple to blue and green to a cool mossy brown. "Whew! I never did that before," she sighed.

"Mommy!" yowled the lion cub. The lioness picked him up by the scruff of the neck and carried him off.

"And that is why lions are frightened of chameleons," Rodentus told his spellbound audience. "When a chameleon gets angry, he turns purple, but when he gets blistering, flaming, boiling *furious*, he turns ultraviolet. Ultraviolet, as we all know from our science classes, is a much more energetic color than blue. It makes it possible for him—or her—to change other creatures. It makes him into a very dangerous weapon, indeed, as the Slopes discovered."

"Listen!" cried Ruva with her ear pressed to the door. "I didn't want to interrupt you before, but it's quiet outside. The weeds aren't moving anymore!"

Twenty-one

THE ONLY SOUND anyone could hear was coming from the air vent. The *Apocalypso* was as still as a ship in a painting. The floor quivered briefly as though it was settling.

"They've stopped growing," said Rodentus, breaking the silence.

"Yes, but what are they doing now?" Ruva asked.

"From the lack of movement, I'd say they've pinned us pretty firmly to the Sargasso Sea. Their roots must be hanging down on all sides."

The floor quivered again.

"What was *that*?" said Jabila.

"This is only a guess, but the vines are probably getting thicker. They don't have to hunt for water so they can just sit there and grow."

"But that means they're getting heavier," wailed Ruva.

"Probably." Rodentus groomed his vibrissae with an elegant paw. The floor tilted slightly.

"We're sinking!" Jabila cried.

"We've got to get out! Boagh!" bleated Ruva. Troll scurried up her leg and perched on her back. The boy put Nelson on his shoulder.

Rodentus dusted off his coat. "What difference does it make?"

"What difference? We're about to sink, you useless creature!" shouted Nelson. "I suppose you want to entertain us with stories on the way down."

"What could you possibly accomplish out there? No one's going to swim a thousand miles to shore. I could improve your education a little in the moments remaining."

"I can't bear being caged!" cried Ruva.

"I know it's useless, but to be in the sun and air—well, it's something," Jabila said.

Even Troll was unwilling to stay. "Please, boss. I'd like to go out fighting. I don't want to be trapped like a rat, if you know what I mean."

"Oh, very well," Rodentus grumbled. "You have an excellent opportunity to learn how to face mortality from one who has studied with the pope and the Dalai Lama. I call it a waste."

No one listened to him. Jabila turned the wheel that sealed the fallout shelter. The door opened to show them a solid wall of Strangleweeds. The boy began hacking at them with Captain Skeekee's knife.

"If you're going to escape, show some intelligence. Pick the largest—that one, I believe." Rodentus tapped a vine as thick as an oak tree. "Cut a hole big enough to crawl through." Jabila sliced through the rubbery skin. The inside was hollow!

"There. That's why they can grow so fast. They're ninety percent air. We'll have to guess how far to walk inside before cutting our way out. Wouldn't want to end up in the water." Rodentus led the way with Jabila and Nelson following. Ruva and Troll brought up the rear.

It was extremely difficult for the little giraffe to move in the tunnel. She had to bend her neck at an uncomfortable angle and practically pull herself along on her knees. It wasn't a position giraffes were meant to take. She was soon tired, but one thing worked in her favor.

The air in the tunnel was delightful. It smelled green and full of life. It made her feel stronger.

"Strangleweed vines are one of the World's major producers of fresh air. They thrive on smog and turn it into grade-A oxygen." Rodentus's voice drifted back to her. "If they weren't so dangerous, I'd plant them all over Los Angeles."

"You sit down and rest, Miss Ruva," whispered Troll. "You weren't made for work like this."

She struggled on, however. The mere thought of sinking while trapped filled her with panic. Finally,

Rodentus indicated a place to cut. Jabila got to work.

They came out onto a scene that was hard to recognize as a ship. Flabby gray-green leaves waved over the deck, the windows, and masts. Ruva gratefully stretched her neck and legs.

They were on a mountain of vines in the middle of a flat sea. The ship's rail was dangerously close to the water. As Ruva watched, the *Apocalypso* shuddered and settled down even closer to destruction.

"If the vines are full of air, couldn't we use them as a raft?" she began. Rodentus held up his paw for quiet. He pointed into the distance.

There—it was hard to see because of the glaring tropical sun—something stirred. Big greasy bubbles floated up. Rank tendrils of slime spread out on the water. As the little giraffe watched, the bubbles came nearer. Suddenly they were all around the ship, and the slime lapped against the farthest weeds. A large glob rose and slid up a vine, trailing nauseous ropes of goo behind it.

Ruva felt her stomach lurch. That color! It was a melting, gluey mixture of sick green and greasy brown, the yellow of old sores and the purple of fading bruises. She swallowed, tasting bile.

"Those, if I'm not mistaken, are the Gross Green Sea-Going Sargasso Snails," said Rodentus.

Everyone watched in silence as the snails ascended the vines. Their long glistening bodies stretched out from under lumpy shells. They had cream-colored eyes surrounded by wet brown rings on the end of stalks.

"You know what those remind me of?" Troll said. "Have you ever looked at the bottom of a parakeet cage?"

"Don't," said Jabila.

As the snails approached, they fed on the plants. In place of teeth, they had vicious-looking rasps. *Scrape, scrape, scrape,* the rasps went, feeding vegetation into puckered mouths.

The snails were not only getting closer, they were growing. New shell was laid down as the creatures expanded. Now and then one of them laid a trail of sticky-looking eggs. In a few moments, these hatched and tiny new snails began to feed.

"Those . . . are certainly . . . *gross,*" faltered Jabila.

"That's the *grossest* green I've ever seen," Troll murmured. "And I used to watch Dante floss his teeth."

"I think we can all agree that it might be nicer to sit in the fallout shelter than be slimed over by snails," remarked Rodentus.

The moment this possibility sank in, everyone crowded back into the Strangleweed tunnel and began crawling for all he or she was worth. Ruva thought she was exhausted, but she suddenly found fresh energy. The very thought of Gross Green Sea-Going Sargasso Snails creeping over her made her

[133]

wriggle with every ounce of her strength. She tumbled out the other end and lay panting on the floor. Jabila sealed the door.

They all lay still for a while. No one said anything. The *Apocalypso* stirred, but this time it went up instead of down. Presently, they heard a *scrape, scrape, scrape* just outside the door. The ship rolled gently. Ruva thought it must have been cut free of all the roots.

No one suggested eating although they were surrounded by boxes of food. No one said anything about what they had seen coming out of the water. Nelson's only remark was "If I'd been out there one more second, I would have lost my mole crickets."

Twenty-two

JABILA INFLATED mattresses from the supplies in the fallout shelter. Ruva curled up on one; Jabila, Troll, Rodentus, and Nelson sprawled on another. Ruva thought she would be too nervous to sleep, but the moment she lay down, she was out.

"Want something to drink?" came a voice. The little giraffe sat up. She must have slept for hours. She felt wonderfully rested. Jabila poured water into a bucket. Ruva was suddenly ravenous. She waited impatiently as the boy opened cans of fruit. Troll had eaten the center out of a chocolate bar and wore the rest of it as a necklace.

Rodentus nibbled a rice cracker. "Good morning," he called cheerfully.

"Is it really? Morning, I mean," said Ruva.

"According to the clock." Jabila pointed to a digital display on the wall.

"You don't need that," Rodentus said. "It *feels* like morning. The sun has risen. The dew is drying on the deck."

"The slime is sparkling on the snails," muttered Nelson.

Rodentus groomed his fur. "As soon as you've finished breakfast, Ruva, we're going to tour the ship. Or, I should say, Jabila's ship. This is a derelict, and the Law of the Sea says it belongs to the first human who claims it."

"This is mine?" Jabila cried.

"You certainly earned it."

"A wreck with a torn-out radio a thousand miles from shore. Be sure you thank him for it," Nelson said.

Ruva was nervous about meeting snails again, but when Jabila opened the door, they were all gone. Only an unpleasant sheen indicated where slime had dried. Every scrap of weed was gone, too, along with everything the plants had managed to devour. Her hooves echoed on the deck.

"They got all the fresh water," Jabila said soberly.

"We have some in the fallout shelter," said Rodentus.

"Wowie! They even ate the carpets!" cried Troll. Nothing was left of the floor coverings except a few balls of fluff. Gone were the curtains. The couches were reduced to bedsprings. Even a few nips were taken out of the floor. These were crusted with dried slime.

"Look down here!" Jabila shouted. He knelt by the hatch. A few rays of sunlight picked out gleams of metal.

"So that was what was in those boxes," murmured Rodentus.

When her eyes got used to the shadows, Ruva saw that the hold was filled with drifts of gold coins. They formed hills where boxes had been devoured by the Strangleweeds. Sapphires and rubies dotted the hills like rare flowers.

"It's *beautiful*," the boy whispered.

Rodentus nipped him on the ankle. "Pupil Jabila, what are you looking at?"

"Why, gold. Money," said the boy.

"And just what is that?"

Jabila thought for a long time. "It's time," he said slowly. "And freedom. Power. It's anything I want."

Rodentus nodded with satisfaction. "You've been paying attention after all. Money is all those things, but most of all it's *I want*. *Wanting* is a demon's favorite activity. You, as a child of Solomon, have to learn the meaning of *enough*. Fortunately, I'm an excellent teacher."

Rodentus climbed down the elevator shaft to be sure the weeds hadn't harmed the cables. "It's safe," he announced. "We can't count on the electricity much longer, though. We'll have to figure a way to start the engines."

"I know how, but I can't run them and steer at the same time," said Jabila.

Gold wasn't the only thing they found in the hold. Some boxes had collapsed to spill out machine guns. "Brrr!" Troll said. "I'd be happy if those went over the side."

The broken faucet was dry as dust. Nearby were a heap of shriveled vines and several large snail shells. Curious, Ruva nosed them. Something scuttled from underneath.

It was Stonewall!

"Boagh! Help!" bleated the little giraffe. The demon cowered against a wall.

Jabila grabbed an oar. Troll's fur stood straight out. "Don't let her touch you, Ruva," the boy said. The little giraffe scrambled up a heap of gold coins and prepared to bring her hooves down if attacked. But Stonewall was in no mood to fight. She curled herself into a ball and shivered.

"What's the matter?" Jabila murmured.

"Look at her clothes," said Rodentus. They were dotted with dozens of little holes. Ruva suddenly understood: the Strangleweeds had tried to devour the cloth, but they must have got some of Stonewall's skin as well. It had poisoned them. That was why there were so many shriveled vines. And the snail shells?

"They ate the vines," said Rodentus, finishing

her thought. He tipped over a shell. A noxious goo dripped out. Stonewall whimpered. It was the first sound any of them had heard her make. It was a horrid noise, like a piece of unoiled machinery.

"I would guess that getting slimed all over didn't appeal to her," Rodentus said.

"Are you going to put a spell on her, Nelson?" Troll asked.

They all watched as the chameleon puffed himself up. His skin turned lavender.

"I don't think I would eat a mole cricket that had once been Stonewall," remarked Rodentus.

"She'd make a good lizard. Try for a Gila monster," Troll said.

"If you rats don't shut up, I won't do anything!" Nelson faded from lavender to gray. He tried again. His eyes bugged out. His skin darkened. Stonewall moaned.

"I can't get mad at something that whimpers when I look at it!" shouted the chameleon. He stalked off to a heap of emeralds and adjusted his skin color to cool green.

"I could lock her in the anchor room," Jabila said doubtfully.

"We're overlooking the obvious." Rodentus stood on a shelf and took what Ruva had come to think of as his professor pose. He cleared his throat and waited for everyone to pay attention. "Here we have a ship that is too large for one boy to operate. And *here*"—he pointed at the quivering Stonewall—"is a perfect dynamo of energy. Observe those muscles, those powerful shoulders. They're made for running engines!"

"But—can we trust her?" Jabila leaned on his oar.

"We can trust her to behave like a demon," Rodentus said with a crafty ratlike smile.

Twenty-three

NO!" YELLED NELSON.

"Wonderful, clever lizard!" warbled Rodentus.

"Why can't someone else be wonderful? Why do *I* get all the dirty work?"

"You're so heroic," cooed Troll. "So noble and brave."

"So snail-shaped," added Rodentus.

They were in the anchor room. The rats had Nelson backed against a wall. Jabila had rinsed one of the shells in seawater, but it still gave Ruva a twinge to look at it.

"All you have to do is pretend to be a Gross Green Sea-Going Sargasso Snail," Rodentus said. "We need someone to bully Stonewall."

"There's nothing wrong with *you*," said the chameleon.

"I have to help Jabila navigate. And Troll would probably do something irresponsible."

"Count on it," said Troll cheerfully.

"You're the only creature with the *courage* and *authority* to order around a demon five hundred times your size."

"I can't help being the only adult in this playpen," Nelson grumbled.

"We're merely rats, but *you're* a direct descendant of Scale and Petal. Lions claw their way up trees when you walk by." Rodentus fitted the shell over Nelson. Jabila had cut holes in it for eyes. "The only thing you must remember is never to let her see the empty shell. She's a demon, but she isn't a complete idiot."

Ruva had to swallow hard to keep from laughing. Nelson looked like a small tank with claws instead of treads. He moved uncertainly with his eyes bugging out the holes.

"You're going to give Stonewall *fits*," said Rodentus. Troll had his tail stuffed in his mouth to keep from giggling.

The lizard lurched along until he found the demon. She didn't think he was amusing at all. She groveled on the floor.

"You! Get to work or I'll slither all over you!" shouted Nelson. Trembling, Stonewall got to her feet. "I want those machine guns over the side. Move, or I might just slime you for sport!"

Back and forth went Stonewall until every gun had been disposed of. Then Nelson got her to work on the engines. The Strangleweeds hadn't touched the diesel fuel. In a short time the ship was able to move.

Jabila stood at the wheel with Rodentus on his shoulder. "I know how to navigate. That's one thing about working for Slopes: they forced me to learn everything."

"Ah! But *where* will you navigate?" asked Rodentus.

"Once I wanted to go to Africa. . . ." The boy fell silent, looking at the waves. They had emerged from the Sargasso Sea, and the water was covered with gentle swells.

"I still want to go to Africa," Ruva said. "I know something about navigating, too." She explained about the mother cat and the Warm Place.

"It's so hot here, I don't know how you can tell one warm spot from another," grumbled Jabila.

"It's a different kind of Warm," the little giraffe explained. "It makes you feel *right*." She closed her eyes and turned. She had been doing it so often, she could find the direction instantly. "There! The grassland where I was born is that way. Mother is standing under a tree, waiting for me."

"That doesn't make sense," said Jabila.

"It doesn't make sense in your head," Ruva said. "It's not the kind of thing you can reason about. Your *body* knows what to do."

"Generally, I have a low opinion of cats, but

that one sounds worth listening to," remarked Rodentus.

So Jabila turned the *Apocalypso* toward Africa. Every few hours he checked with Ruva to be sure the direction was correct because Africa is a big place.

As the days passed, Jabila perfected his skills as a sailor. Rodentus gave him lessons in etiquette. "Start with the utensil farthest from you," he said, tapping one of the forks by the boy's plate. "Salad first, then the main course. The one on the inside is for pie."

"What good is all this? I'm going to be a sea captain."

"You are a child, pupil Jabila. No one will believe you own this ship unless you act like it."

"What good is a pie fork without pie?"

"There's chocolate pudding in the Meals-Ready-to-Eat. Kindly make do."

Jabila found sails stored in the fallout shelter. Nelson bullied Stonewall into running them up. "No point wasting fuel when we have wind," Rodentus said. The ship moved steadily east as the demon ran here and there to ease off a sheet or secure a hatch. Nelson plodded after her breathing threats.

At night she was locked into the anchor room with a pile of Meals-Ready-to-Eat. Ruva noticed, with an unpleasant sensation, that even the aluminum plates were gone by morning.

"This is the life, Miss Ruva," sighed Troll. They were all lying on the deck with the stars shining overhead. Water slapped against the hull with a comforting rhythmic sound. Troll rested his head on a macaroon from one of the Meals-Ready-to-Eat.

"We're very close to home," the little giraffe said. "I can feel the grassland inside."

"Good. I'm getting sick of that snail shell," muttered Nelson. Jabila brushed off dried slime that had sifted onto the lizard's scales.

"Then we have to make plans," Rodentus announced.

"Not now!" groaned the others.

"It's such a beautiful night. Why can't we relax?" Jabila said.

"Because we're almost out of food. We have an extremely dangerous Slope on board, and you're dressed like a cabin boy on a garbage scow. Any crook we might meet onshore would throw you overboard without a second thought."

"I hate it when you're logical," said Jabila.

BY THE next evening, they were close to land. A breeze blew from a dark forest across the water. The lights of cooking fires gleamed here and there among the trees. Not far to the north, a large city glowed against the sky.

"Time to go shopping," said Rodentus. He and

Jabila slipped off in the lifeboat with a sack of gold coins. Ruva watched anxiously as they disappeared in the dark.

"I expect they'll be knocked over the head the minute they arrive," Nelson said, but the two returned before dawn with an amazing collection of purchases.

Next morning Jabila stood on the deck of the *Apocalypso* as Stonewall brought it into port. He was dressed in a royal caftan and wore a gold-embroidered cap. He carried the fly whisk of an African king. All the gold and jewels had been hidden in grain bags stacked in the hold.

Tradespeople came on board with furniture, food, and the other things a wealthy prince might need. For Jabila was now Jabila Al Salami, crown prince of Tiburon.

"Where's Tiburon?" asked Nelson as he dragged the snail shell around after Stonewall.

"It's a town I used to see across the bay when I lived in San Francisco," Jabila said. "It was beautiful and green, but I never had enough money for the ferry."

Stonewall carried boxes, moved couches, and hung curtains. Soon the *Apocalypso* was as fine as it had ever been. In the afternoon, officials from the city came out to pay their respects to the visiting prince.

"This is pretty good," Jabila whispered to Rodentus as he was presented with bowls of fruit, flowers, and other gifts.

"Don't let it go to your head," murmured the rat. When everyone went home, the *Apocalypso* sailed a short way from shore. Troll strung Christmas-tree lights from the masts.

How they partied then! They had rice dotted with raisins and almonds. They ate mangoes and papayas. Ruva was given a bouquet of acacia leaves. Troll frolicked in a bowl of chilled caviar. Nelson feasted on termites, and Rodentus toasted them all with a cup of green coconut juice. Jabila set off Roman candles he had bought in the city.

"Hurrah for Prince Jabila of Tiburon!" shrieked Troll as the fireworks roared into the sky. A splintering crash below made everyone jump.

"Is it a rocket? Are we on fire?" cried Ruva.

Rodentus leaped to the top of a deck chair. "Nelson, where's your snail shell?"

"I forgot about it because of the party. *I left it in the anchor room!*" groaned the lizard.

Everyone stood perfectly still. The fading sparks of the Roman candles fell into the water. Something large ripped out the last shreds of the anchor room door and rapidly climbed the water pipes.

"Uh-oh," said Troll.

They all watched Stonewall climb out of the hatch. She hurled something at the door of the captain's cabin. It bounced and rolled not far from Ruva's feet. It was the snail shell. *Be water, be wind,* whispered the giraffe ancestors in her ears. She faded from the demon's view.

Be wood, be wall, whispered the rat ancestors to

Troll and Rodentus. Nelson faded into the shadows, but Jabila was perfectly visible. Ruva leaned toward him.

"You know how to *disappear*," she said. "Your body knows." She despaired of explaining it. Then, suddenly inspired, she added, "It's like the Common Speech."

Stonewall was so angry, her toes sizzled and her eyes glowed like red-hot marbles from a furnace.

Ruva saw presences move behind Jabila. They were like the giraffe ancestors clustered around her. They were human and yet much, much more. They put out shadowy hands. Tallest of all was a man in a dark blue robe. He wore a crown and his beard curled over his chest. *Be earth, be sky*, whispered King Solomon into Jabila's ear.

All at once, the boy faded away. He *disappeared* exactly like an animal!

Stonewall raged through the ship when she couldn't find anyone to fight. With one powerful wrench, she snapped the ropes that held the lifeboat and hurled it into the water. Then she dived in after it. Steam boiled up around her body.

Ruva saw her climb into the boat. Steam still rose from her skin, but she had cooled enough not to set the wood on fire. She grasped the oars and plied them with all her furious, demonic strength. The little boat shot out across the water and was swiftly lost to sight.

"She's heading for shore, about five thousand

miles in the wrong direction. That's one stuuuuupid demon," said Rodentus.

The spell was broken. Ruva could see everyone again, including Jabila, who looked dazed.

"Wowie! She scorched the deck," Troll cried. Black footprints led across the wood to where the lifeboat had been.

"I understood what you meant, Ruva," Jabila said in a wondering voice. They all turned to look at him. "The Warm Place. *Disappearing.* My body already knew about them, like the Common Speech." He turned slowly around. "I feel something out there. . . ." He burst into tears. "It's my mother! She's waiting in the old apartment for me to come home. I haven't thought of her for a long time. Oh, I'm such a selfish, ungrateful person!"

"There, there," said Troll. "Mothers are very forgiving. They're used to kids acting like rats."

"You couldn't help being a prisoner," Ruva said.

"I've been pretending to be Prince Jabila of Tiburon. It's just a stupid act!"

"It's an act, but not stupid," said Rodentus. "You need it to command the sailors you're going to hire tomorrow."

"But I'm not a prince or a sea captain! Everyone will know I'm a fraud."

"How do you think anyone learns authority? By acting until it becomes real. Pull yourself together, pupil Jabila. You have a lot to learn. Besides"—Rodentus grinned—"those sailors have never heard of Tiburon. A baby rat could fool them."

Ruva heard Rodentus's voice as he strolled along the deck with the boy: "On the way home I intend to give you more lessons. You must learn the uses of banks and—most important—when *I want* should turn into *enough*. . . ."

Jabila sighed deeply.

The little giraffe was far more interested in finding a bed. She had learned all she really cared about: *her* home lay straight ahead across the dark shore of Africa.

Home Again

RUVA AND NELSON said good-bye to Jabila and the rats on the beach. Above, the newly hired sailors were lined up in fine new uniforms on the deck.

"I'm so close to Africa, I ought to visit," Jabila said wistfully, "but now I know Mother is waiting for me. I'll come back someday."

"I had hoped to rid the World of Slopes," said Rodentus. "Oh, well. The Dalai Lama always said I poked my nose in places it didn't belong. For all I know, the World needs Stonewall running around in it."

"I'm going back to the zoo," said Troll. "Shall I give the Gila monster your forwarding address?"

"Get lost," growled Nelson.

Jabila, Troll, and Rodentus returned to the ship.

Its whistle blew a long good-bye. Then the gap of water between it and the shore began to widen.

Ruva and Nelson watched until the *Apocalypso* was only a smudge on a hazy horizon. The little giraffe turned to be sure of her direction. The chameleon climbed onto her back and clamped his toes onto her fur. "Let's go, sweetheart," he commanded.

Ruva arrived in the grassland on a cool rainy morning. She put Nelson down gently on a rock, where he faded into the pattern of granite and lichens.

Her relatives were standing under trees. Mother trotted forward to greet her. "Ruva! How wonderful! You escaped—but you're so tall!" They rubbed noses.

Ruva had grown. When she left, she could barely reach the lowest branches of the acacia. Now she stood level with the trees. But in all things except size, the grassland was exactly the same. The buffalo still turned into patches of shade with Buffalo Magic; the hippos became rocks with Hippo Magic. The fish eagles floated overhead, and the cane rats— so like Rodentus but without his nobility—pattered beneath. It was all as it should be.

"Darling, it isn't polite to *disappear* in front of family," Mother whispered.

"I'm sorry. I didn't know," replied Ruva. She became perfectly clear: brown spots and tan fur, dark eyes and velvet nose. She became perfectly clear: hoof, horn, and hide.

[152]